P9-DFQ-201

FIRST DAY ON EARTH

FIRST DAY ON EARTH

CECIL CASTELLUCCI

 SCHOLASTIC PRESS/NEW YORK

This book was written in part with a fellowship from the MacDowell Colony.

Library of Congress Cataloging-in-Publication Data available.

ISBN 978-0-545-06082-0

10 9 8 7 6 5 4 3 2 1   11 12 13 14 15 16

Printed in in the U.S.A.   23
First edition, November 2011

The text type was set in Adobe Caslon Pro.
Book design by Kristina Iulo

TO THE FARTHEST STAR
WITH THE KINDEST HEART

We are all in the gutter,
but some of us are looking at the stars.

—OSCAR WILDE

1.

You think you know what I am, the kid slumped in his chair in the back row, with greasy hair, wearing all black. You're kind of scared of me. 'Cause I'm a loner.

But you don't know shit.

We are specks. Pieces of dust in this universe. Big nothings.

I know what I am.

I am a guy who loves the human race. I love us. I wouldn't hurt a fly.

Did you know that I help people? Even when they don't ask but they need it? Mothers and their baby carriages on staircases. Old people. Homeless people.

You ignore them. I don't.

Did you know that I'm a vegetarian?

Did you know that I rescue animals?

No.

You think I'm scary-looking.

You laugh behind my back. I know it. Don't deny it.

Because who cares what you think about me?

With what I've been through, I just shrug it off.

But in case you're interested in what *I* think, here's what *I* think about you.

You think that you're something. You think that your dumb teen problems are so big and important. You think that who's popular in school and who wears and says the right thing is important.

It's not.

You're ignorant. Asleep.

I've been to outer space and back again. I've been caged. I've been probed and spliced and diced and I am being tracked. They are going to take me again one day. I know it because I heard them say it in my brain. They are out there and they are watching us. And you just move like a sleepwalker from class to class whenever the bell rings.

I think you are sheep.

But one day, I'm going with them. And I'm going to be free.

2.

I've got a towel around my hips. I'm waiting until the showers are a little less crowded before I step into them. I'm not shy. I don't care about being naked with the other guys. I just like to have a little space. Josh likes to shower with a lot of other guys at the same time. Maybe he likes to look at the other guys' dicks. Maybe he compares them. Whatever floats your boat, I say. Life's too short to care either way.

Josh and his friends emerge from the showers. They're laughing and they move to the corner and start getting dressed, putting on deodorant and talking about girls in a way that I don't like.

"What kind of guy are you?" Josh asks. "Tits or ass?"

"I'm a tit man, for sure," Colm says.

"When my girl Posey jumps, I swear it's like watching a door open in heaven," Josh says. "Her tits are like peaches, only not fuzzy."

"You've touched them?" Colm says. "I bow to you."

"Sure, I've touched them," Josh says. "They kind of belong to me, right?"

"Right," Colm says. "Posey's tits are yours for the touching."

"Technically, they are not. Technically, they are her tits," Darwyn pipes up. Darwyn says it kind of matter-of-factly, like he's been part of the conversation the whole time. Even though he's really just sitting near the guys who are talking. They tolerate him, but he's not their friend.

"I'm thirsty," Josh says.

And Darwyn, big doughy Darwyn, sees that as an opportunity to move closer into the circle. I watch as he debates with himself for a minute, sort of looks down at his feet and figures it out. I see him do this all the time. Decision made, Darwyn gets up and goes over to the water cooler and fills up a cup.

I notice that his black skin glistens a bit from the water that is still clinging to him from the showers. He looks like his body has been bedazzled. I've seen something like that—the water-like diamonds—before. But the memory of it is just at the edge of where my conscious mind ends.

"What are you staring at, Mal?" Josh says, his attention now on me. "Are you hot for Darwyn? Oh my God. Mal has a crush on Darwyn. I always knew you were gay."

He laughs and his friends laugh. I look at Darwyn, who is standing by the cooler, a little cone cup in his hand. Gold-rimmed glasses a little fogged up. Big fleshy arms, jiggly belly. He's frozen there, like he doesn't know whether or not Josh saying that I'm gay means that Josh is saying that Darwyn is gay.

I look away. No one here would care if I was gay or not. And I actually don't care if I'm gay or not. Being gay might be better than what I am now.

"Hey, Darwyn," Josh says. "Can you help me with my car after school? It's making that funny noise again. I thought we could go to your dad's garage and take a look at it."

Darwyn breathes a sigh of relief that his status hasn't been affected by my unwanted staring. Darwyn's willingness to do anything and everything at all times for anyone gets him kind of in, even though he's out.

The showers are empty. The bell is about to ring. I consider not showering, but I smell from shooting hoops by myself. And I never have deodorant on me.

"Dirty pig," I hear Josh mumble under his breath as I pass him. Colm and the others laugh. But not Darwyn. Darwyn only laughs after a few seconds. He's just following.

I've heard worse things said about me than *dirty pig*.

The words run off my shoulder as I walk toward the shower.

3.

Sometimes I have a rage inside of me. Like a lion roaring. Like a firebomb. Like a white-hot piece of metal. Like a train wreck as it's happening.

It gets so bad that I can feel every single cell in my body writhing in pain. Like a pin pushing into each part of me. Every inch hurts. Every pore screams. You cannot imagine.

On those days, when it gets bad and I can't stand my mom crying on the floor in her pajamas anymore, I go out in our shitty car and drive to the desert. As soon as I see the windmills, I pull over and climb out of the car and stumble up toward them. The air is crazy. All swooshing and electric. I feel as though I'm a piece of machinery that has been suddenly set to full throttle. And there's a noise. Not a noise that sounds like anything else you've ever heard. It is a whirring whisper with a purr. It is steady and magnificent, the windmills capturing energy right from the sky.

I stand underneath those windmills. I stand there and I scream. I scream and scream until I don't have any more voice in me. My soul sails out onto the wind, or up into the blades, transformed into raw energy. Most times I have destroyed a shrub or two with my fists, not even feeling the parts of the leaves that prick like needles and get under my skin because, like I said, I already have needles pricking me everywhere.

The screaming it all out makes it better for the drive home.

But that feeling of calm never lasts for long.

4.

The lights in the sky don't lie.
The lights in the sky don't lie.

5.

"Mal?" Mrs. Yegevian says. "Which poem will you be sharing with the class?"

All the bodies in the room turn in their seats to look at me. I don't like their eyes on me. I've had too many eyes staring at me.

I stand up. My hands shake as I hold on to my notebook, as though it is going to keep me steady.

"Mal?"

I clear my throat. My voice is hoarse.

"Pass," I say and sit back down.

There are snickers. There are always snickers. Kids who cover their mouths with pretend sneezes as they say *loser* under their breath.

Mrs. Yegevian says nothing, but leans over her notebook and puts a mark next to my name. Another black mark. I have so many, I don't even try to clear my name anymore. No one expects me to.

Alphabetically, Posey Manitsky is next. She stands up without being called to do so. She is so sure of herself. How did she ever get that way? Does she wake up with sunshine and rainbows streaming through her window? Does she smile so naturally because everything is so good? Because she sleeps like she's an enchanted fairy-tale princess? Must be. No other explanation.

She throws back her shoulders and swings her long hair out of her face. Her hand is steady as she reads from the paper. Her voice as clear as a bell. But I'm not noticing all that. I'm wondering if her tits are really as peachy as Josh says they are.

Her honey tones fill the room as she reads her poem.

> *I think the strange, the crazed, the queer*
> *will have their holiday this year . . .*

"What the hell was that?" someone says when she's finished the whole thing. "Did she just say *queer* and *gay*?"

She gets snickers, too. The kids here are equal opportunity snickerers.

"Tennessee Williams," Darwyn says. His desk is at the front of the room, as always, facing Mrs. Yegevian's desk. He's her special helper. He hands out the exams and collects them. He keeps attendance. Takes extra notes. He always knows too much and doesn't have the sense to keep the extra information he's acquired to himself. "Tennessee Williams: best known for his plays, such as *Suddenly Last Summer, Cat on a Hot Tin Roof,* and *The Glass Menagerie.*"

"Shut up, Lung," someone yells. That's what the cool kids call Darwyn behind his back and to his face. Lung. 'Cause he talks too much and is compelled to overshare.

Darwyn winces at the nickname. He pushes his glasses up, even though they haven't slipped or anything. He purses his lips. He looks up at something on the ceiling. His index finger points up. Like he's showing us something up there. I think maybe he'll start to cry. That'll be like blood in the water. They'll rip him apart if he does that.

I am actually worried for him.

But he doesn't cry. He just keeps staring at the ceiling.

I look up there. There's a water stain near the sprinkler. It's in the shape of a bat.

"Tennessee Williams," he says quietly. More like he's talking to himself than to anyone else. "A great American playwright."

The whole class is howling now. Well, almost everyone. Not me. Not Posey. Not Darwyn. Not the two shy kids near the window. Not Mrs. Yegevian.

"Settle, people. Settle," Mrs. Yegevian says.

Someone else reads a poem. A stupid one. It sounds like a Hallmark card. My poem would have been better than that.

I look down at the poem that I chose.

e. e. cummings, (once like a spark).

My poem. More *real*.

The bell rings. And I do what I do best.

I get the hell out of there.

6.

"Is that you, Mal?" Mom is slurring her words. She's got the box of wine on the counter and she's probably halfway through it already. Probably already three sheets to the wind.

She's listening to an oldies station. They're playing grunge music in the flashback-at-five section.

Nirvana — "Smells Like Teen Spirit."

In here, it smells like sour grapes.

"It's me," I say.

I picked up some food from Subway for dinner. I put it on some plates and get some paper towels. I pop open the can of Coca-Cola and slide it into her hand, replacing her cup of wine. She doesn't argue.

"I have to go to group," I say.

There is always a meeting at the community center if I need to get out of the house.

"Okay," she says.

I bet if she sobered up, she'd look pretty. I bet if she hadn't been crying every single day for years, she'd be pretty. I bet if she'd gotten an explanation for why he left, she'd be pretty.

I finish my sandwich, put my dish in the sink, and then head outside.

I hop on my bike and head to the community center. On my way, I do a few tricks. I mess up, but no one is looking at me.

It'd be faster if I drove. If I drove, I'd have more time to do my homework. But gas is too expensive and we're on a budget. Besides, riding my bike keeps me out of the house for longer.

And I don't do my homework anyway.

7.

Our Alateen group leader is looking at us with his soft eyes and serenading us with his caring tone of voice.

"Who wants to share?"

I raise my hand.

"Mal?"

I tell the story again. Like I always do. I have told the same story a million times.

"He said it like it was nothing. 'Better get some milk tomorrow, we're out.' 'I can get some,' I told him. 'On my way home. After school.' 'No, Mal, I can do it in the morning,' he said."

And then I go on and tell the whole thing.

That before I woke up for real that morning, when I was just waiting for the alarm clock to ring, I heard the front door click. Softly, not like other times when Dad left in the morning and the door just closed in the background, but as though someone were deliberately trying to be quiet. That's what made it so loud. It was *weird*.

I remember looking out the window. The morning was gray. Maybe there was fog. Or maybe my memory is foggy. He had his brown corduroy coat pulled on. His porkpie hat on. And a suitcase in his hand.

If only I had been more awake, I would have realized he was leaving. Maybe I could have said something. Could have persuaded him not to go.

Instead, I put my head back on the pillow and tried for five more minutes of sleep.

"You know it's not your fault, Mal," our group leader says. "Your father was gone. He was incapable of staying. It has nothing to do with you. Neither does your mom's drinking. It has everything to do with them."

They say these things to me over and over again. But it never makes any sense.

8.

There is a question that I always ask myself. I ask it many times during the day. How far away from here is far away enough? How far away would I be willing to go?

My answer is always the same.

You? I bet you'd think the moon was far away enough.

I say the moon is still too close.

Here's the thing with the moon. You can still *see* it. Mars? Too recognizable. Jupiter is too stormy and everyone is always looking at Saturn's rings. Maybe Neptune. No one ever knows when Neptune is around. It just sits in the sky, disguised as a star.

But those aren't the places that I'd go to. Those places are still too close. I've got my eye on something farther away than that.

Mr. Cates is discussing Human Migration.

He underlines it on the whiteboard.

Human Migration

I look out the window, letting Mr. Cates's voice recede to a soft buzz until I can't even tell what language he's speaking anymore. I stare at the moon.

It's sitting there, in the sky, even though it's morning and the sun is out. It just hangs there, showing its face. Begging to be lived on.

Mr. Cates passes us a handout. He's pointing to the board. He's talking about how history changes. Times change. Things change. What was once unacceptable becomes accepted. What was once accepted becomes unacceptable.

"People, they leave the terrible behind. They leave the people who don't understand. They leave because they're burned out. They leave for a better life. They leave the way things are, for the way things could be. They start over. They go across the ocean. They discover new lands. They settle the West. You can call them whatever you want—explorers, conquerors, settlers, pioneers," Mr. Cates says.

He dims the lights and starts up an animated computer slide show that demonstrates the movement of people from place to place. The colors go from one end of the earth to the other. I am transfixed by the swirl of colors.

I think some people go just because they have to get away.

I think that they were lucky back then. To have somewhere that far away to go. Somewhere totally different. Somewhere totally unknown. Somewhere they could disappear. Somewhere with breathable air. A place that wasn't even mapped yet—the edge of the world. I'd have signed up for that so fast I wouldn't have even packed a bag.

But these days, where can a person go? Not even Antarctica is unpopulated anymore.

The only place to go is up.

"Every day is different," Mr. Cates says. "Every day is a new day in history."

The only thing that is different about most days for me is the weather and what class I'm going to fall asleep in.

The bell rings and I'm the last one out. I don't care if I'm late. No one cares if I'm late. I move through the hallways slowly, as though time doesn't exist. I pick my way through the pressure of bodies. Gravity gets heavier as I enter English. Everything slows down when everyone looks up at me standing in the doorway. I try to be quiet as I make my way to the back of the room.

It takes me forever. Luckily, I know all about how ten seconds can feel like a year.

After English, I am walking behind Darwyn and his bigness that takes up even more space than is physically allotted to him. Darwyn does not move slow. He moves fast. He's happy to be bumped into or to bump into others. He buzzes from one person to another. He uses the time between classes as an opportunity to talk to people, especially people who don't want to talk to him at any other time.

"Hello, there!" he says. He smiles. He waves. Then I watch as he trips on his shoelace. He is like a big rock in the middle of the hallway, forcing the stream of bodies to part and then come together again. People are laughing as they pass by him, and as I move closer, I can see why. Everyone can see his butt crack. At first he's laughing, too. But then I can tell that he's distressed. He doesn't know how to fix the situation and is trying to play it off as a joke. Darwyn tries to tie his shoe, hold his books, balance his heavy backpack, and pull down his too-small shirt. No matter how hard he pulls his shirt down or his pants up, it will not cover the butt crack. It is an impossible task. I go over to him and take the books out of his hands.

Darwyn stands up.

The hall is now empty.

The late bell rings.

"Oh, no," he says. He's actually worried about things like being late for class. It matters to him.

I give him back his books.

He takes them and runs down the empty hallway, turning to disappear down another hallway.

I am standing alone, wondering when I'm going to bother getting to science.

I ask myself that same old question.

How far away from here is far away enough? How far away would I be willing to go?

Light-years.

9.

I'm in the Albertsons, putting milk and cheese and bread and spaghetti into the cart. The wheel is stuck.

I curse.

I'm on the ground, trying to see what the problem is, when I hear them talking about me.

"That's Lucy's boy, isn't it?" a woman's voice says.

From where I am fiddling with the wheel, I look up and recognize her, from the now-distant time of barbecues and picnics, games nights and playdates. I almost smile. Because sometimes just making a connection in your brain makes you smile. But then I stop because why should I smile at her? At them?

It was worse a few years ago, after Dad left. I'd be in the supermarket, picking up food because Mom wouldn't even leave the house. Now it's just habit that I'm the one who does the shopping. But back then, when I was eleven, I was confused. I thought they were talking *to* me, not *about* me.

The look on their faces, the crazy poofy hair, the piled-on makeup, the smoker's rasp as they whisper—it's inhuman.

"Yes," the woman next to her confirms.

I remember their names. Susan and Jessie.

Whenever I run into them, I always hear them going on and on. It's a variation on the same theme.

"It's a shame about Lucy—"

"Well, she did it to herself. Just let herself go—"

"Obviously weak—"

"No wonder he left her; she was a mess—"

"She's crazy—"

"He was right to walk away—"

"He was so nice. Always so polite. A good husband—"

"Better than mine—"

"She just hates herself. Who could love someone who hates herself so much?"

"He was a great guy. She was lucky he stayed as long as he did—"

"She's the crazy one. I mean, look how she acts—"

"You know I tried to reach out to her a few years ago. But she was still screaming about it. And now, a drunk—"

"She looks ancient—"

"I feel sorry for the kid—"

"Tragic—"

"Well, we all have our lot to bear—"

"Such a mess. Such a terrible mess."

No matter how quickly I try to get out of there, I always hear a part of it.

I forget about the stuck wheel and about the food in the cart and I head out of the store, leaving those women and their wicked, awful words behind me.

Those women, the way they talk about her, that's what's *really* crazy.

You would never know that they used to be her friends. Her best friends.

There isn't one friendly thing about them.

10.

My life sucks.

So I shave my head.

11.

"Hey, why do you always look so angry?"

The girls are all around me. One of them is twirling her hair. One of them is chewing raspberry-flavored gum. One of them is picking something out of her nose ring. One of them is painting her toenails.

It's free period and we're supposed to be studying. I'm reading a book that has nothing to do with anything we're learning in school. Mark and Sameer, the only two people that I'm kind of friends with, are sitting too far away from me to be of any help. They don't notice anyway. They're the kind of guys who never look up. They've got their buds in their ears and their noses in their books. We're all reading books.

Mark is reading *The Web Coder's Technical Manual*.

Sameer is reading *The Body Builder's Guide to Beefing Up*.

I am reading *The Undiscovered Self*.

I don't say anything to the girls. I just hope that they will go away. All the girls at school look the same to me, except Posey. She looks different.

"He's got such a bad vibe," one of them says.

"You are so angry," another one says.

I'm *quiet*.

"I can't believe they don't just kick you out of school."

"Or that you don't quit. People like you usually just quit."

I look for Posey. A lot of the time, she shuffles them away from me. She makes it so that they get distracted by something else. But she's absent today.

Maybe my jaw muscle is twitching.

Mark and Sameer surprise me by looking up. But they don't really know how to help me. No one can help me.

I look out the window. The sunlight slants through the columns outside the window. It highlights the dust in the air.

The girls continue to cluck. But they sound far away. Their voices sound slowed down. There's only the window and the dust and Mark and Sameer gone back to reading their books.

I do like they do. I go back to reading.

Always solace in a book.

Always silence in there.

12.

I find the kitten on the side of the road, mewing like it's the end of the world. His mom is dead, her guts pouring out of her belly, and two of his siblings are dead, too. But here is this one little runty thing, still alive. Mewling and tiny. This one was smart enough not to follow the others into the street. He lost his mom and he knows it. This cat knows that he's all alone in the world.

I know all about that. It's a painful thing to know.

"Hey, little guy, I'm here," I say. I'm careful when I pick him up. He's so tiny that he fits into my jacket pocket. As soon as he's snuggled in there, I can feel him relax. He starts purring against my body, purring like a hacksaw, like a hallelujah. I can't help but smile.

I wonder if this is how they felt when they found me.

I do what I always do when I find a lost animal. I bring him to the Del Vista Street Animal Shelter.

"Hello, Mal," Dr. Manitsky says when I come in. Dr. Manitsky is Posey's mom. Today she's wearing a light purple scrub outfit with pictures of Winnie the Pooh floating off on a balloon. "Who do you have for me today?"

I lift the sleeping kitten out of my pocket and hand him to her.

She takes him carefully and places him on the exam table. The little thing wakes up and starts to wander around on the metal table. Dr. Manitsky keeps scooting him back so she can finish what she's doing.

"New haircut?" she asks as she takes the kitten's temperature. She's not even looking up to stare at my bald head, like other people do. I reach up and touch it. I like the way the stubble feels.

"I guess," I say.

"Thinking about college yet?"

"Just thinking," I say.

"That's good," she says. "Posey's wanting to go out east. She's considering Brown. I keep telling her that's far from home, but I guess we all have to go on our own way one day. Even if that means going far away."

"I guess," I say. There are days I can't imagine leaving home. There are days it seems like something impossible. Like I'm in a cage that looks like a house.

But then I remember. I escaped from here once. Maybe I can do it again.

Dr. Manitsky starts to baby-talk to the kitten. "You're such a pretty little thing, aren't you? Little handsome devil. Going to catch someone's heart."

She's scratching his back and the kitten is purring away, like he finally knows that everything is going to be just fine. That there is still love in the world despite a dead mother in the middle of the road. Despite being all alone.

I wonder if this is how I felt when they found me.

"So is the cat going to be okay?" I ask.

"A tough guy like this? Sure thing, if all his tests work out, he'll be adopted for sure," she says.

"I don't like to think of him being all alone," I say. I don't like to think of *anything* being all alone.

Dr. Manitsky looks at me like I'm one of the animals in the shelter. I don't like it when she looks at me like that. Somehow, it's worse than the women in the Albertsons.

I am not an animal.

"You and your mother should come over for dinner sometime," she says as I follow her into the back to watch her put the kitten into one of the cages on the wall. He sniffs around his new home, eats some kibble hungrily, and then goes to the corner and falls back asleep.

"Oh, I don't know," I say. As though I'm seriously considering it, which I'm not. I never consider it when she asks, which is practically every time I come by. We're watching the little guy as his chest moves up and down. I'm amazed how his belly, which was flat and bony before, is now suddenly big from eating. Just a little bit of nourishment makes all the difference.

"Well, I know Posey would love to have you," she says.

I know that Posey wouldn't mind, but I hardly think that she'd love for me to come over.

"My mom doesn't really like to go out much."

"You could always come alone."

"I don't like to leave her by herself. She doesn't remember to eat."

"You can visit Flopsy. I'm sure she'd like to see you."

She's talking about the rabbit that I rescued from the elementary school when I was in sixth grade. It was the first time I rescued something. One of the kindergarten teachers had forgotten him in the parking lot. I went there on that Saturday, after school had closed for Easter vacation, to practice popping the wheels on the dirt bike I'd gotten for my birthday. I saw the cage sitting there in the empty parking lot, on the sidewalk in front of a faculty parking spot. The rabbit inside was hardly breathing.

My dad had just left, and seeing that rabbit just about killed me.

I took the rabbit out of the cage and ran out of the parking lot with him, leaving my bike behind. I ran and ran, even though I didn't even know what to do or where to go. I remember blind panic. I thought I had to hold him and love him and save him. And when I was running, I saw the animal shelter and came inside and Dr. Manitsky was there, in her scrubs. She looked up from behind the counter and saw the half-dead rabbit in my arms and she knew just what to do. She stuck an IV in him and she let me pet him as she helped him come back to life.

I said I'd ask my mom if I could take him home. But when I got there, things were bad and I never asked her, because how could I take in a rabbit? It was ridiculous. The next time I found an animal that needed rescuing, I brought it in to Dr. Manitsky, and found out that she had taken Flopsy in herself. She said I could have him anytime. But that rabbit reminded me of before. Even though it happened after. I never asked for the rabbit. And until today, Dr. Manitsky never mentioned anything about it. Which made me feel relieved.

Sometimes I thought it might be nice to see Flopsy again. Like it would be some kind of test of my strength. But it wouldn't do to go over there. I know I would just become a blubbering idiot.

"Tell Posey I hope she feels better," I say.

"You can tell her yourself—she'll be back in school tomorrow."

I head out of there, and as I bike toward the setting sun, wind whipping smoothly along my new aerodynamic head, I wonder why Dr. Manitsky is so nice to me.

The pocket feels extra empty without that little cat. I want that kitten to be my kitten.

But I remember the same thing I always remember when I drop off a rescue at the shelter. A rescue that I might want to keep for myself. What if I go to college? My mom would never be able to take care of a cat once I left.

She can't even take care of me.

She can't even take care of herself.

13.

I know where he is.

He has a new family. He lives in Victorville.

And I hate him.

14.

When he was around, we used to do things together. He'd pile stuff into the car and say, "Come on, Malcolm! Are you ready for an adventure?"

And I'd get excited and have to go pee an extra time before we left.

I'd sit in the front seat. It would be just me and my dad. I'd stare out the window at the landscape as it passed by. The brown dirt. The palm trees. The outlet stores. The scrub.

We'd go somewhere cool, like Joshua Tree, or Angeles National Forest, or even the Grand Canyon once. We'd pitch a tent and eat adventure food. Beans in a can. Hot dogs. Trail mix.

We'd lay our sleeping bags out on the hard ground and we'd look up at the stars.

"That's Hercules," he would say. "The strongest man in the world."

"Because he was so big?"

"Sure, but that's not the only way a man can be strong. He can look weak and little and be stronger than a tough guy on the inside."

I imagined that my dad was like that. Even though he was slight on the outside, he seemed big to me.

"There's Cassiopeia—she hangs upside down half the year because she was so vain. . . ."

I thought of my mother. And her long blond hair. How she wore it loose around her shoulders. She was beautiful, but never vain. She used to be an actress when she was young. A child actor. She showed me the sitcom she was on for two years before it was canceled, and the toothpaste commercials she'd done.

But no one wanted her when she got older. Except for my dad.

"What about that star? Why is it moving?" I asked.

My eyes were trailing a star that had suddenly emerged brightly and then started to move sideways.

"Where?" my dad asked, and he leaned over to follow my finger pointing up at the night.

"Is it a UFO?" I asked.

"That's a man-made satellite," he said.

"How do you know?"

"There are so many satellites orbiting the earth now, that if anything was out there, close to us, I bet we'd know about it."

I watched the star as it moved away and then suddenly blinked out.

The last time we went out there, it was the November before he left, and there was a meteor shower.

We lay there staring at the sky blacker than anything, with the Milky Way stretching like an unconcerned spill. And the sky looked alive. The stars fell faster than the wishes I could make.

I wish I had a better bike.

I wish I was three inches taller.

I wish I could grow a mustache.

I wish I could be in Mr. Jeter's homeroom next year.

I wish I had a better video game system.

I wish.

I wish.

I wish.

Now I think that was childish. I shouldn't have wished for anything dumb.

I would have been better off wishing for better things.

Like a heart for my dad.

Like that he would never leave.

Like to know how to make my mom feel better.

I would even have added world peace in there while I was wishing.

What I don't know is whether I would have wished for them to leave me alone.

15.

I have my head down, so I don't notice at first. And pretty much every meeting goes the same. I just walked into the wrong room. Or it's the wrong day. Or they changed the meeting room. Or it's a spooky coincidence. This time, when the group leader asks someone to share, I hear something that sends chills down my spine.

"My name is Devon and I am a contactee," a little guy says.

"Hi, Devon," everyone says aloud.

"I was first taken when I was a small child. The aliens were reptilian in nature. They told me that they had a right to probe me. It was their right. . . ."

I feel a little faint. Like I'm going to throw up. Not because what the little guy is saying is weird. But because it sounds so *right*.

I want to run out of the room.

But I don't. I swallow some of the piss-poor coffee. It hits my stomach like a shot of battery acid. I clench. But the coffee helps.

I sit and listen. It's toward the end of the meeting. When Devon is done, Earl, the group leader, gives everyone tips for handling the fact that they've been abducted. He says that he has been taken his whole life. Over and over again. That there's a girl who he's paired with and breeds with. He says that he's never met her on Earth. And that she doesn't speak English. She's Swedish, or Finnish, or some kind of country like that. He knows that because she looks like Pippi Longstocking. Or a Viking. He says though he's never met her, if he saw her in the street, he would know her. He says that whenever he's in an airport, he looks around, scanning the crowds, wondering if he'll see her. He never has, even though he's traveled a lot.

I bet there's a mathematical equation for that. One person in California and one person in Sweden and the odds of meeting someone on a planet with more than six billion people.

In a way, I am kind of jealous of Earl.

He wraps up the meeting and everyone files out of the room. But I'm still sitting in my chair. My mind is racing.

At first nothing I'm thinking is coherent. Thoughts burst like summer lightning in my brain. It's so random, and scary, that I'm sure that my synapses will explode into an unmanageable fire.

All this time, I knew I couldn't have been alone. But somehow I was. And whenever I tried to look for others and to reach out, it seemed so silly. How could a person sift through what was real and what wasn't real out there? Part of me always believed that if it had happened, then they would come and take me again. And that would prove it. But they never did.

That's when I began to doubt myself.

Of course there were people who were just plain crazy. Who made it up. Who were crying out for attention. And I already had doctors saying that I was crazy. I didn't want to add to it. So I never said anything. I just hinted. Hoping that someone would say, *"Oh, yes. That could be what happened."*

But now, I had found others, and to them there was no question. It was real. The way Nadine shook when she talked about the Atfatfatf and the way they turned colors depending on their mood. Or the way Earl looked like he really missed that lady. Or the way Devon talked about the reptilian men made me think I wasn't crazy.

But what scared me, what made me feel like I would explode, was that if it had happened, then I couldn't sometimes pretend that maybe the doctors were right and I was crazy. Maybe I had a hallucination. Maybe I had wandered all that way on my own. Maybe I was too sad.

Because like everyone in the room said, there is no evidence. There is no proof. There is only this weird feeling, sitting at the edge of your memory.

After listening to everyone speak, I feel embarrassed. Because now I know for sure that I had never had to be alone.

I squeeze my eyes shut because something is breaking through, right up to the surface. Then, in my brain, there is a buzz and a hum and it feels familiar and not scary. So I relax into a calmness that I haven't known in years.

I know what I'm going to do.

I know that when I'm ready, *I'm* going to share.

16.

Before and after is how things are divided.

17.

It had been eight months since my dad had left.

It was a little bit cold for the beginning of July. I remember I rubbed my arms to get warmth into them. My mother was over by the sausage truck. She was drunk, and no matter how many times she tried putting the sauerkraut onto the bun, she kept missing. There were little piles of kraut by her feet. I was embarrassed.

There was a man selling sparklers. He wore a hat. It wasn't a porkpie hat. It was a cowboy hat. But it triggered something inside of me. Like, who was this man, standing there, casually selling sparklers? Smiling. Having a good time. I didn't know him. But he had a little boy with him. His kid, who he kept touching on the head. And leaning down to smile at. There was so much love there.

Whenever the little boy got a little too far away from the man, the man would remind him that he was right there. That he wasn't going anywhere.

And I think I broke.

Right then.

There was this stinging in my eyes. And this swell of salt. I had been numb for what seemed like an eternity. Sitting on my front porch, looking out the window, waiting and hoping that my dad would come back.

Surely he was going to come back. Surely he wasn't going to leave me there, with my mother on the floor. Surely he wasn't going to leave me all by myself.

And there, watching that man with those stupid sparklers, I knew for sure, my dad wasn't ever coming back. He didn't care at all. He could be standing right in front of me and he could see how much I hurt and he wouldn't care.

I looked back at my mom, the sauerkraut at her feet. The dog only half eaten but two big cups of beer next to her on the table. And I imagined that if I felt this bad, she felt a million times worse. And suddenly it was like there was a piano sitting on my chest. The only way to breathe was to walk, to make sure that oxygen was coming into my body. So I started to walk. But I couldn't see which direction I was going in. I just kept walking. I didn't have a flashlight. I tore my pants. The stars were so bright that I could swear they were changing colors. And then the fireworks stopped. I couldn't hear the voices of everyone gathered to watch them. I was winded. I was farther away from anywhere than I'd ever been before.

I knew that there were scorpions and rattlers all around. And I was too heavy. My limbs were so heavy. My eyes so heavy. My heart so heavy.

I dropped to the ground.

Ready to die.

But instead, the lights came.

They were small at first. And then they came.

18.

There are kids everywhere on the lawn, on the sidewalk, on the stairs, at the picnic tables because it is fifth-period lunch. I am sitting by the flagpole next to a garbage can, by myself, eating a peanut butter and banana sandwich. Josh and his boys are at the picnic tables right in front of me. The boys are trying to pinch the girls who are with them. Posey is sitting on the ground. She is eating a roast beef sandwich. There is mayonnaise on her face.

Darwyn is sitting on the ground between me and them. It looks like he might be with them. But I know he's not. That's where his spot is, though.

I'm close enough to observe everything. It makes me glad to not have friends.

"Hey, Darwyn," Josh yells. Darwyn perks up at the sound of his name.

"Yes, Josh?" Darwyn says, and takes it as an invitation to move just a little bit closer to that special circle.

"We're going to have a party at my house next Friday night," Josh says. "My parents are going out of town for the weekend. You can come if you bring the beer again."

Darwyn brightens.

"I can get some from my dad's store," he says. "No problem."

"Outstanding," Josh says. Posey gets up, maybe to throw away her napkin. Josh takes his legs and squeezes them around her, to trap her. She laughs and pretends to beat him away. Finally, he lets her go. She goes to the garbage can. She picks up something else that didn't make it in and places it in there, too. I like that she sees things like that.

"Bring more beer than you did last time," Josh says. "Loads of it."

Darwyn nods his head a couple of times. Then he looks at me for confirmation that he was really invited. Because he assumes that I must've heard it.

I give him the thumbs-up. He gives it back to me.

He doesn't go back to reading his book. He just stands around, hovering. Laughing with the group. Interjecting here and there. And today they're encouraging him. So he's going on and on about something or other.

Right now I hear them doing trivia, and Darwyn is answering every question right. Sometimes they treat him like he's an idiot savant.

And they laugh right at him, right in front of him, right in his face, and they say, "Lung knows it all!"

I can't remember the last time I ate lunch with someone. Mark and Sameer never eat outside. They say that it depresses them too much. They eat in the library. But I like the sun. The sun is a star. I wonder what constellation we're in.

It seems strange to sit here and listen to Josh and the other kids share everything that is boring and mundane when all I want to do is talk. But if I do, I want to talk about big things and big ideas. Not about parties that I don't want to go to. Not about what trivia Darwyn knows or doesn't know. I wonder what would happen if I went right up to them and shared the news that there are people walking around who have bigger, more interesting things to consider. Things like the fact that there is probably life on other planets and they are visiting us here on Earth.

But then I freeze up. Because even allowing that thought to be fully formed in my head makes me feel kind of sweaty and sick.

Today the only things that want to share anything with me are a plastic bag that is stuck in the garbage can and a squirrel making off with someone's Cheeto.

19.

Chem class.

"So our hypothesis is incorrect," I say.

"Are you sure? I don't believe you," Suki says.

Suki is chewing on her pen cap. She does not want to be my lab partner. Neither does Natalie.

I've got the beaker in my hand.

My hand is shaking.

Sometimes when I look at the beakers, it makes me nervous. Being in a lab brings something back up, some half-remembered memory inside of me that I don't like.

Experiments. It seems unbelievable to me that school teaches us to be the experimenters. The observers. The prodders. The measurers. The destroyers.

We are never taught what it would be like if the tables were turned.

We are never taught what it would be like if we were the rat in the maze.

Or the frog on the dissecting table.

Or the atom being split.

We don't like to think about that.

We like to think that we are being civilized.

I'm not so sure what science means anymore. Part of it seems beautiful and part of it seems monstrous. After all, how can we understand the unknowable without experimentation?

How could they understand anything about us without seeing what we are made of? I can't blame them for being curious. For wanting to know what makes us tick. I am curious about them, too.

Then I think about a cold, hard metal table and I close my eyes for a moment.

At least we are not dissecting anything this year. I had to take a D in biology because I couldn't handle the bio part. I just couldn't handle those frogs, those pig hearts, pinning the skin back and reaching inside.

"Just write it down, Suki," Natalie says.

Suki leans over on her stool to ask Posey at the next lab station, "Hey, what did you get?"

"Correct," Posey says.

"That's not what we got," I say.

"It's not?" Posey checks her notebook. "Are you sure, Mal?"

"I'm sure," I say.

"Well, he must be wrong," Suki says.

"Who cares?" Natalie chimes in. "We still get a B for completing the lab."

"Wait," Posey says. "Wait."

She leans over and rechecks the work of her group.

"I see—it's a trick!" she says. "Mal's right."

I start disposing of the chemicals. I suppose I could feel smug. But I don't. I'm just glad that science speaks for itself so I don't have to.

"Hey, Nat," Posey says. "Can I go to your house to hang out before the party? I don't want to go all the way home."

"Sure," Natalie says.

I wipe down the lab station.

"There's a party tonight, Mal," Posey says. "It's at Josh's. You can come if you like."

I see Suki roll her eyes. Which means I'm not really invited.

"Everyone is invited," Posey says. This is not a pity invite. She's making sure I understand that I'm welcome. "Even your friends."

I don't bother to tell her that I wouldn't really go to a party with Mark and Sameer. But they're okay to sit with sometimes. They're pretty okay guys. Regardless of what the truth is, it's thoughtful of her to include them. "Thanks," I say. "I'll think about it."

I think about it for exactly a nanosecond.

No.

20.

I am thinking a lot about what I know. I know how big the ship was: 250 meters. I heard them talking about it. I don't understand how nobody else saw anything that big in the sky. Maybe everyone is blind. Maybe no one ever looks up. They just take the sky for granted.

You'd think that it'd be in the newspapers, or online, and people would blog about it and shit, but I check every day and there are never any reports of UFOs. Well, sometimes in other places, but not in my town.

I figure

a) they have some sort of stealth technology.

b) there is a government cover-up.

I'm not crazy. Not like I suspect some of the other people in group are. Like this guy Greg, who wears a tinfoil hat and says he gets messages in his teeth. Not that there is anything wrong with that. I mean, who am I to judge?

If I thought that tinfoil would tune me in or block me out, I would totally do it.

It's now my fourth meeting. I'm slouched in my chair. I still have not shared. The other group members are talking across one another now, and arguing. There are about ten people in the group tonight, and they're all older than me—some of them much older. There's only one guy, a new member, who could possibly be a teenager. He's sitting across from me, as quiet as I am. He says his name—Hooper—when it's time for the introductions, which is the only reason I even know his name at all. He's interesting to look at, so when I listen to the other people speak, or when I zone them out, I watch him.

His hair is curly and a weird kind of blond except for the tips, where there are hints of black. It doesn't look dyed. When he turns his head to the side, he seems to be much older than I am, like an old man, but when I look at him face on, he looks young. At first I think he has no eyelashes, but I realize that they are just translucent. They make his eyes look much bigger than everyone else's. He smiles at me. When he smiles, he looks extra goofy.

"What are your aliens called?" Earl asks Nadine, the woman who's sharing.

Someone stifles a yawn. Maybe a laugh.

"I don't know," she says. "It's not like they were chitchatting with me. They were *probing* me."

"Well, usually they say something, like 'We are the Martians' or 'Klexians' or 'Malolians!' 'Greetings, earthling!'" one of the other guys, Harold, says.

"Be cool," Earl says. "No one laughed at you when you shared."

"I don't want to share anymore," Nadine says.

Hooper plays with his long fingers the whole time. It's like he's never seen fingers before. He wiggles them and examines his nails. Feels the knuckles. Makes a fist. Clasps his two hands together. Flips them open and over and examines his palms.

He sees me staring and stops what he's doing. But I can tell it's hard for him because he sits on his hands. Then he looks at me and kind of laughs, like he can't keep from looking at his hands for long and knows it. I wiggle my fingers for a little while so he doesn't feel alone. Or stupid.

I don't like it when I feel stupid. And I'm pretty sure that no one else does, either.

At the end of the group, Earl looks at me when he asks if there's anybody else who wants to share. But I can't do it. I can't tell whether everyone else in the room thinks I'm a fake, that I'm just some kid getting off on their weirdness. But here no one ever pushes. Maybe because we've all been probed before. Or maybe they realize that I get it. Maybe there's some kind of radar where you can tell when another contactee is in the room. All I know is that listening to them talk makes me feel safe.

Hooper comes over to me after group when I'm unlocking my bicycle.

"Hello," he says.

He says it weird. Like he doesn't have much practice using his voice or his tongue.

"Hello, Hooper," I say.

"Mal," he says.

"That's right."

"*Mal* means bad."

"Yeah," I say. "In Latin. Or French. Or Spanish. But I'm not Spanish. And I'm not bad."

"No," Hooper says, like he's sure of that, even though he doesn't know me.

"It's short for Malcolm," I tell him. In case he wants to know. He nods.

"Mal," he says, and then he looks up at the sky and wanders away.

Malcontent
   Mal du siècle
   Malediction
   Malefaction
   Maleficent
   Malevolent
   Malfeasance
   Malformed
   Malfunction
   Malice
   Malign
   Malignant
   Malnourished
   Malodorous
   Malpractice
   Maltreatment

22.

I got lost and disappeared.

For days.

Sometimes I wonder which part of me came back.

23.

Mom is lying on the couch. She's got the TV on low. I'm sitting with my laptop and I'm doing homework.

She starts snoring.

After he'd been gone for two years, my mom finally got enough money to do the surgery, but ever since then, she snores.

She believed that if she had the perfect nose, my dad would come back. She thought that maybe it would help. He always used to say that she was beautiful except for her nose. He said that her nose ruined her perfectly good face. Then she would cry. Then he'd take it back and he'd hold her and say that it was okay, that she had other things about her that were good.

Sometimes he'd say to her, "I know you'll leave me one day." He'd be crying a little bit. I could hear them through the door, and Mom would swear on her heart that she never would.

"I love you," she'd say.

He promised her that he would never leave her. Never, ever. He swore.

And then they'd coo and coo and get quiet except for the grunting.

I never remember him saying that he loved her back.

24.

I hop on my bike. I think maybe I'm just getting out of the house to get some air. Or a Thai iced tea. Or to get away from the flickering television and the take-out boxes that I don't feel like cleaning up. Away from the smell of sour wine. Away from the homework that I don't want to finish. If I had gas money I might go to the desert. But instead, I'm on my bike. My legs pumping. The wind making the dry heat cool.

I go down one street. Pass another. Make a left at the gas station. Make a right at the bottom of the hill.

And there I am.

Josh's party.

Someone is throwing up on the lawn.

There is underwear and toilet paper in the tree.

I lock my bike. I don't want any of these cool kids to steal it. Even if it's beat-up, it's still my bike.

I don't rush inside. I go slowly. I figure I'll just inch in there. Check it out. I'm already regretting finding myself here when someone throws an empty beer can at me. I duck inside the house.

As soon as I get in the door, someone puts a drink in my hand. He's wearing a peacock headdress. I'm not sure why. Maybe he's on drugs.

I sometimes wonder why they took me when there are so many other stellar specimens of how fucked up humanity can be. Then again, in group, the one thing that strikes me is that everyone seems so incredibly normal. Well, almost everyone. I know that they didn't take me for what I knew. Because at twelve, what could I possibly have known about anything? Except that people leave with no explanation.

Then again, so do aliens.

On the couch, there are a bunch of people making out. They keep switching who's kissing who. I turn away and head to the kitchen. Josh is in there slicing up limes for tequila shots and asking who's up for one. I catch eyes with Darwyn, who's sitting at the butcher-block table. He's like, "Yeah!" But he doesn't say it as strongly as the others.

Someone hands me a shot. I lick the salt. Take the shot. Bite the lime. It's pretty good. But I pass on doing another.

I go to the back porch. There are a bunch of girls dressed like weekend hipsters and they are giggling like crazy. There's a cat hissing at them.

"Mal." Posey says my name when the cat screeches by me in an attempt to escape.

"Hey," I say.

Natalie comes up to me and dances all slow. Like some dance she saw in a movie or a TV show on how to be sexy. Only it's really not sexy.

"Well, I just thought I'd stop by," I say. "Since you invited me."

"Cool," Posey says.

I wonder why she's nice to me. Is it because her mom works at the pound and is the one who checks in all the lost animals I bring in? Maybe she's supposed to be nice to me. It doesn't really matter. Nice is nice.

Suki slips her arm around Posey's waist the way girls do and whispers something in her ear. They both turn to each other and away from me.

I wander back through the party, saying hello to the few people that I talk to on occasion and having interesting conversations with some kids from another school. By the time midnight rolls around, the party has gotten too big and too loud for me, so I bail.

But I'm actually glad I went. It wasn't as bad as I thought it was going to be. Every now and then, it's good for me to get a sense of how everyone else lives. In case they come back and ask.

25.

The papers arrived when I was fourteen. I was the one who picked up the mail. The return address was from a lawyer. The envelope was thick.

My mother screamed when she saw it.

And then, when she was done screaming, she called everyone she could. Begging them to make it not true. Begging them to tell him to change his mind.

He didn't care what had happened to her.

What he'd left behind.

This mess of a woman.

This woman who was my mother.

Me with all the pieces, broken and un-glueable.

He was happy where he was. He was *happy*.

He just wanted to get rid of us so he could move on.

He had moved on.

But we had stayed.

He was never coming back.

He was never looking back.

I found my mother on the floor. A bottle of pills next to

her. I called 911. And stroked her hair and sang songs to her until they came and took her away and pumped her stomach.

26.

I want to be taken away from here.

27.

On Monday, as I pass by some of the kids who I talked to at the party, they jut their chins out at me in a sort of weird, passive hello. The thing that's weird is that I know they don't really want to talk to me or anything, but now I'm full of things that I want to talk about.

My secret is blowing up inside of me, but now it doesn't hurt.

I almost feel high. Or what I imagine being high is like. Despite what you probably think, I've never been high. But right now, I feel euphoric. I'm *happy*. Almost crazy happy, but it's because I feel like I want to burst. I have to keep putting my hand over my mouth to stop myself from blurting things out. Or maybe it's to hide the fact that I'm smiling so much.

Hanging by the lockers before first period, Sameer and Mark look at me like they want an explanation. But I don't say anything. I just take my textbook down off the shelf in my locker and put it in my bag.

We start to move together down the hallway to our classes, and I want to put my arms around their shoulders in happiness. I want to squeeze them and tell them that everything is going to be okay. Not because I know that it is, but because I feel so relieved about everything. Because I am not alone. *We* are not alone.

As I'm about to peel off from them to go up the stairs to the second floor, they kind of stand there and look at me. That's when I notice it. They have a look in their eyes. It's a look I haven't seen them give me before, and I don't have to be able to read minds to know what they are thinking.

Sometimes, silence is very loud.

Their feelings are hurt. And I am the reason.

"I guess I should have asked you guys to come to Josh Nelson's party," I say.

They kind of shrug. But from the way they shrug, I know they agree with me.

I feel like a bonehead. I wouldn't survive these halls every day if it weren't for them. We are the reason why none of us ever has to be alone in a sea of people who don't understand us. But just like I could never tell them about the sky and what happened to me, I can't tell them that I need them to get through each day.

"You didn't miss much," I finally say.

"Yeah," Sameer says.

"That's not the point," Mark says.

A part of me is surprised that they even care about something like Josh Nelson's party. But that's something else we never talk about—parties, or school, or feelings. And since we talk about nothing, I know nothing.

I have to make it up to them because even though they don't say anything, they're mad at me. But I don't know how to fix it.

So instead, we just stand there, our eyes darting around, not really falling on each other.

"I gotta go to class," Sameer finally says. He adjusts his backpack, and he and Mark go on their way.

I watch them walk down the hall, admiring how they stick out as being so different from everyone else.

It hits me that I have never even told them that, and I doubt I ever will. All the happiness that I felt just hisses out of me. I'm like a deflated balloon and it's not even nine.

I'm back to everything being like it always is. Back to feeling as though nothing will ever change unless I say something.

I have to say something to someone.

28.

I decide it's time to share.

"I'd like to share," I say.

"Go ahead, Mal," Earl says. And then all eyes are on me. I feel a bit parched. I take a sip from my water.

Hooper is across from me again. He's looking at me and his eyes never seem to blink. It makes it hard to read his expression. But he seems interested for the first time I've ever noticed. Then again, he also seems interested in his fingers.

This guy Greg smiles at me, encouraging me on. Like it's going to be all right if I tell my story.

So I look up at the ceiling and I start to talk.

"I was twelve. It happened right out there in the desert on the Fourth of July," I say. "They said that it was only fireworks in the sky that night. But it wasn't. I know that."

The others start nodding. I don't have to feel silly about what I'm saying. They've been there. Or somewhere close to it. They believe me.

29.

It was loud and bright, with webs of fire falling all around me. And then the light embraced me, like a kiss. It kissed me and it felt so warm. The light was singing to me. It lifted me off the ground where I'd lain down to get a good look at the stars. My back arched and it felt like all my bones were snapping. But they weren't. I went into the light. It lifted me up. There were hands all over me. Small, moist hands. They pinched me, and the sting of it felt like fire ants biting me up and down my body. They were taking something essential from me. Something from my insides. The light was so bright and the instruments they used to hold me down were cold.

They were gray. Little gray men. I swear they were gray. With big eyes. All pupils and no color. That was how I knew that it was like I said and not like what everyone else thought. Those eyes had no color.

I never saw their mouths move, but I could hear them. The words were meaningless but I knew that they were talking about me. It was a swarm of sounds inside my head. I remember thinking that listening to a song in their language would be painful.

But after a while, even painful things become familiar, and so I let their incomprehensible words push through me. I spent most of the time with my eyes closed, my lids too heavy to open. I think I was drugged but still conscious. Every part of me was being tugged on. When I could open my eyes, the light was too bright. That light pierced me, and my eyes refused to make sense of what I was seeing. But I knew I was a slab of meat floating on a bed of metal, with that buzzing inside my head and those hands and instruments all over me.

That didn't mean much, until later, when I started getting flashes. Of hallways and cages. Of one of them taking my hand and patting it, like it was trying to comfort me. Of another one explaining unexplainable things to me with words I could not understand. Of being given a hot liquid meal that tasted like yerba maté. But I can't ever call up a fully formed memory. Not much comes to mind except the brightness and the certainty that something happened to me. It's more like a *feeling*. With eyes.

The police found me in the dirt three days later. Nowhere near the fireworks. Miles away from the town. How do you explain that?

You can't.

Some people think I ran away. But I didn't. I didn't even know that it was three days later. I thought I'd been gone for an hour.

I didn't walk to the desert. I didn't like walking that much, not when I was twelve, so I definitely wouldn't have walked from Indio all the way to the 62 highway. I just wouldn't have. They put me there. They put me back close to where they thought they found me. Hell, from space it probably is like exactly where they found me. 'Cause when you've come a million light-years, what's a mile or two?

But no one believed me.

They said that maybe I didn't run away, that maybe I had a seizure. That I had some kind of brain attack that made me walk for miles in the desert on a hot summer night and stay there for three days. They said they knew that something was up because of my brain waves. Because of the levels of stuff in my muscles. Because of the bruising consistent with a seizure of some kind. They said that it fit that I smelled burnt toast the whole time. They said that my life had been full of trauma and that it was just a psychotic episode.

But that didn't explain the weird scoop in my leg. I tried to tell them that I'd never had a hole like that in my skin before. They didn't count it as new because it looked all healed up.

They put me on drugs to keep me calm.

But I don't take them anymore. 'Cause there is nothing wrong with me.

And I know what I know because I know.

30.

I wipe my hands on the sides of my pants and look around. Everyone starts to clap.

"Thank you for sharing," Earl says. He gives me the thumbs-up. Then he moves on to the next piece of business. He reads from an alien abduction handbook.

I have just shared and it's like nothing has happened.

Greg is picking at his Styrofoam cup. Nadine is blowing her nose. Hooper is looking at the clock.

"It's almost time for the meeting to end," Hooper says.

I can barely hear him because I start shaking. I'm not cold or anything, but my whole body is trembling. I wonder if maybe I'm having a fit. I wonder if I should be worried.

I want to cry.

I've shared a million times about my dad and mom in my Alateen meetings or group therapy and I've felt nothing. But here, telling this story, it's like showing my most secret parts. It's like being naked. It's like being at your ugliest and that being no big deal.

I wonder if it's that what I said is just so normal to everyone here that there's no need for a reaction. Or if it's just that no one here really cares about anyone else's story. It's hard to know what's true.

I take the back of my sleeve and wipe my now-wet eyes and running nose.

I am surprised when Hooper puts his hand on my shoulder. He's close to me and he smells. It's not a good smell or a bad smell—it's a weird animal smell.

"Steady, Mal," he says. "Steady."

And then Earl says his final words and it's time to go.

Outside of the community center, other people from the group mingle and linger on the steps. They are talking easily, laughing and making plans. Greg is debating Earl about the finer points of SETI. Nadine is making movie plans with Devon. None of them come up to me and ask me any more details about what I said. Secretly, I'd be glad if one of them came over to me and compared their abduction with mine. But all of our stories are not the same.

I look up at the sky.

How many ships are up there?

Or are there none at all?

I climb on my bike and pedal hard, getting the rhythm of the wheels to move faster than the speed of my thoughts.

When I get home, my mom is passed out on the floor. The TV is on. And for the first time in forever, I don't help her up off the floor and steer her toward her bed. I leave her where she is with the TV still on.

I just want to go to bed.

Sharing has made me lighter.

Sharing has made me tired.

31.

To make it up to Mark and Sameer, I agree to go to the movies with them on Saturday. We are at the mall waiting for our movie to start. We have an hour to kill, so we're sitting silently in the food court. Mark is playing a game on his iPhone. Sameer is reading a thick-ass urban fantasy book. And I am staring at remnants of the molten belly bomb of a pizza I just devoured as though there is a worm living in my stomach.

For all I know, there *is* a worm living in there. An alien parasite. Perhaps I'm a host.

We're going to see a disaster movie. There's going to be a tsunami, an earthquake, a volcano, and a flood. The special effects are going to be awesome. The sound is going to be extra loud. Which is funny, because here we are, a bunch of guys who love loud movies, and yet we are the quietest teenagers in the mall.

Even when we occasionally gather at Sameer's to play video games, we're quiet. When one of us wins, we don't yell or whoop or give each other noogies. We just nod triumphantly. Like we don't want to show off. Or we're sorry that one of us is the alpha male for a minute.

I look over at the other table, where there are a bunch of teenagers I don't know who are horsing around. They behave exactly the way you think normal kids horse around. They kind of wrassle with each other. They laugh, as though they are so together. A unit. A group. My eyes shift, and I see them as a monster, one body with a bunch of different heads. When they move, they do it together, as one being. None of them individual in any way.

Maybe that's what's wrong with Mark, Sameer, and me.

We're in our own bodies. We're uniquely ourselves, with no clue how to be in a group.

On the other side of the food court, I see Josh, Colm, Suki, and Posey. They behave the same way, like a group monster. Although, as I study them carefully, I notice that Posey looks like she's trying to separate. It's as though she has one foot that's her own that keeps trying to step out in a different direction. But she's not succeeding, and they keep pulling her back in.

———

After the movie is done, we walk back to my car, sipping the rest of our sodas and making small comments about the film. We debate about whether or not the director has lost his touch or if he's kicked it up to a new level. Sameer votes kicked it up. Mark votes lost his touch. I remain neutral.

I bet that Josh and his group all think the same thing. No dissenting voice.

We go back to Sameer's and order more pizza and play more video games.

Sameer's parents come in to tell us to turn down the volume, and we do.

We don't have a conversation about anything other than the game we're playing or the movie we're watching or the song we're listening to.

I wonder what they would say if I told them about my mom, who is most likely drunk and passed out at my house. Or about my father and how I want to punch him in the face. Or how I cried like a baby when Dr. Manitsky had to put a puppy I found two months ago to sleep, because it was so sick that it was kinder to kill it. Or how I was abducted by aliens four years ago.

I look at Sameer, the light from the TV smoothing out the acne on his face, and Mark, whose ponytail looks historic. And I wonder what's bursting inside them.

After losing the battle in the game for the fourth time, I pass my controller over and get up to leave.

We never know how to say hello or good-bye, the three of us. It's always been a bit awkward.

Tonight when I get up, I rub my hands on my jeans. And then I shake each of their hands like I'm an ambassador from another planet mimicking human customs.

Sameer smiles, and nods, and I know he's impressed that I've solved a simple human puzzle.

Hello and good-bye are not as simple as everyone thinks.

32.

It's raining really hard. I see a dog trotting down the street. I slow down my mom's car and follow it. It's obviously lost.

I roll down my window and call to it.

I whistle.

It stops and looks at me. It's panting. It's a big golden retriever. That dog's got a great smile. I stop the car and I open the door. I call the dog in. The dog looks at me. Looks down the road.

It starts trotting again.

I follow it.

That's when I see him.

Hooper.

He's in a box in the underpass staying out of the rain. The dog goes right up to him and Hooper puts his hand out. The dog lies down at his feet. I pull up and park and get out of the car.

"Hooper," I say.

"Mal."

"Is that your dog?"

"This dog?"

"Yeah, I thought maybe it was lost."

"It is probably lost. This dog does not belong to me. But it is a nice dog."

"I was going to take it to the pound."

"Good idea, Mal," Hooper says. Then he says something to the dog. The dog gets up and comes trotting up to me. I open the back door of my car and the dog goes in and lies down on the backseat. Totally comfortable, it closes its eyes.

"Do you live here?" I ask Hooper.

"When it's raining," Hooper says. "This large structure protects me from the elements."

"Are you hungry?"

"Sometimes," he says.

"Do you want to go get a burrito?" I say.

I don't know if he has any money.

"My treat," I add.

Hooper smiles.

"Let me get my things, Mal."

He gets his little backpack. It's got lots of pockets and it's very high-end. So are Hooper's shoes, I notice.

He gets into the car and sits very still as I drive to Juanita's Burritos.

33.

I think Hooper might be a crazy homeless person.

We are sitting at Juanita's, me and Hooper, and Hooper is on his fourth burrito. He's got salsa on his shirt. He's chewing with his mouth open. And he looks like he's in heaven.

"Taste is very interesting," he says between bites. "This one with the beef is very different from the vegetarian one."

I keep sipping on my soda while he goes on about the differences between the burritos that he's sampled.

"And the different kinds of salsa. Mild. Medium. Hot. It's quite brilliant."

I'm not afraid of people who other people think are crazy. My mother is crazy and I'm not afraid of her. She just sees the world differently than other people. For her it's a suspicious place, full of darkness and disappointment. Like the very light of the world doesn't exist anymore. But Hooper is full of excitement. He's crazy in a different way.

I want to ask him about his abduction. I want to ask him if he really thinks that it happened to him. But I don't, because I think maybe that might be rude. There might be a reason he's never volunteered anything in the group. And also I don't want him to start talking crazy, like so crazy that it's something that I can doubt happened to me.

As much as I like some of the people in the group and think that they totally believe that what happened to them happened, some of them seem unreliable. Like Julie, this woman who is convinced that the aliens keep impregnating her. That she's got fourteen children growing up on another planet. Or Laird, who has the broken iPod that he receives transmissions on. Or the woman who came once and proclaimed herself the Queen of Mars, then never came back to another meeting.

But Hooper seems different. He seems like when he finally shares his story, everything that happened to me is going to make some kind of sense. I don't want him to be unreliable.

For right now, I keep quiet and dissuade him from buying another burrito. The last thing Hooper needs is to get the runs in his box under the freeway.

I don't feel comfortable bringing Hooper back to his box under the freeway. But I don't know what else I'm supposed to do.

He's dead asleep beside me. It takes me a while to shake him awake when we get to the place where he "lives."

"It's fine," he says. "I am better there. More space to think."

I let him out and he goes back.

He sits in his box.

I sit in my car.

I can't press the gas and leave.

I roll down the window.

"Hooper," I say. "I think there's a shelter next to the pound. Can I take you there?"

"A shelter?" he asks.

"You know, a homeless shelter."

"There are such things?" he asks incredulously.

I might have to accept that he's totally crazy. I nod.

He gets up, checks his area, gathers some more things, and gets back in the car. The dog barks once, happily.

Hooper helps me take the dog to the pound. And then we get him checked into the shelter.

"Thank you, Mal," he says. He's got tears in his eyes.

"No problem," I tell him.

I get into the car and I hum a little as I drive away. I feel pretty good about myself.

When I get home, my mom is sitting at the kitchen table and she's happy that I brought her a burrito, her favorite kind.

When my mom smiles, when the clouds break up enough to let some of her sunlight come through, it's like old times.

Tonight, she gets out the Scrabble board.

Today was a good day.

34.

There are so many animals in the pound. The young ones, the puppies and kittens, are cute, but the old ones, toothless or limping, are cute, too. They're all in cages, just looking at you like they can't understand what they've done to be locked up like this.

I know exactly how they feel. Even on the good days, because I know that good days only last a day.

Maybe it would be better to be free.

Maybe if I wished on enough stars, those aliens would come back and take me with them. It might be better to be an experiment. Maybe I could do good for humanity by being probed. Or maybe those aliens would be so smart that they could take the part of me that hurts so much and cut it out of me. They can have the part that makes me feel so bad, the part that makes me think that sometimes I can't put one foot in front of the other. And maybe if they did that to me, and returned me to Earth, I could point them to my mother. They could take her up in their spaceship, and use those instruments on her and give her some peace.

Because surely if they can fly all the way across the universe, to our galaxy, to our solar system, to our planet, then they must be very advanced. They must know things. They must have some kind of answer.

And if you have an answer, then pain can go away.

Because it makes sense. It's understood.

If my mom could understand. If I could help her to understand, then maybe she'd go outside again. Face the sun. Drink it in. Lift up her arms and twirl. She would maybe laugh, and all the brown dead plants in the garden that she has forgotten about would turn green again. And bloom.

They must have a ray gun for that.

I often wonder where the tracking device—if I have one—could be inside of me. How small it is. If skin and muscle are growing around it. If it just looks like a tumor. I wonder if there is anything I could do to shut it off.

I wonder why aliens would care about me.

And if they do care about me, why did they leave me?

35.

Why is the hardest question in the world to answer.

36.

She's in the living room. It's the day after our good day. She's got her hand splashed over her forehead, like she's got a headache.

"Mal," she says as I come into the room and put a plate of spaghetti down in front of her. "I don't know what I'd do without you."

"Well, I'm sure you'd do fine," I say.

"One day you'll go," she says. "One day you'll go to college. Be a man of your own. Have a family. I'll be forgotten. I'll be all alone."

I don't know what to say.

There is a thread that goes from me to her. It's a lifeline. Only it's not keeping me alive.

Maybe if I got far enough away to snap it, she'd take the trash out on her own. Remember to eat more than just one meal. Wash her face. Take her pills. Start going to talk to someone.

Maybe, if I was so far away she could never find me again, then she'd hit rock bottom and start to climb out of this mess.

37.

Hooper doesn't show up for group again for a couple of weeks, and when he does, he seems like a different man. He's cleaner, more put together. The thing about Hooper is that cleaned up and happy, he looks like he's about seventeen. But he must be about thirty. The other thing that is different about him is that he doesn't look like a crazy homeless person. He looks like a regular guy. But he still smells weird.

After group, he comes up to me.

"Mal!" He's very excited. "I would like to take you out for a burrito," he says. When he grins, his smile looks wrong. His teeth look like baby teeth, as though he never lost them. They are sharp and tiny and make his young face look even younger. It distracts me for a moment, but then I snap out of it.

"That's okay," I say. "You don't have to buy me one. But I'll totally go with you."

"No, I insist," he says. "Burrito is now my favorite food."

On the way to the parking lot, he tells me about how they found him a room, with a bed and a lamp and a sink with running water. And he's got a little job in the kitchen at the shelter.

He gets into my car and he gives me all kinds of weird directions until we end up far out of town, at the foothills of the Sierra Madre, where there are wide-open spaces, horses, and tumbleweeds. There, in the middle of nowhere, is a taco truck. Like a real-deal taco truck. He walks up to the guys, who wave and call out "*Hola*, Hooper" to him.

Then he orders in fluent Spanish.

"You speak Spanish?" I ask.

"They speak Spanish," he says, pointing at the men and women working the taco truck. A few weeks ago, he didn't know what a burrito even was, much less how to say it. Now he speaks with a more pleasant accent than my Spanish teacher.

We eat the burritos and mine is the best burrito I have ever tasted in my life.

The sky is clear and the moon rises. There is a bright star near it.

"That's Jupiter," Hooper says. "No life there. Only here."

"Yeah," I say.

We stare at the sky for a while, because there's nothing that's more beautiful than the night sky. I remember, even though it hurts, that I learned all the constellations by name because my dad started teaching me them and made it seem like it was something that he'd finish doing with me. Like the night sky was only for us to share. And now, we can't. After he left, that first year, I learned them all on my own. I went to the library and took out a book on it, just so that when he came back I'd be able to go out into the desert with him and impress him with my celestial knowledge. For a while there, learning those constellations by myself was like having him still with me. I would imagine how when he came back, he'd be so happy that I had loved him that fiercely. He'd see how special I was and he wouldn't want to leave again.

But it's been almost six years and he hasn't come back, even though I just about killed myself learning all of those constellations. All for nothing. And no matter how hard I try to forget the patterns in the sky, I can't.

I get that feeling in my chest. The one where I feel the hurt inside of me like an extra organ that was put in my body the wrong way.

I look up at Cassiopeia. It's the easiest to spot. Like a *W* hanging in the sky.

Why begins with *W*.

"Do you ever wonder where your aliens came from?" I ask.

"My aliens?" Hooper says.

"The ones who abducted you? I mean, I look up at the stars and I wonder, which one is their home? Why did they come here? Why did they take me?"

I don't say the other thing that I always wonder about my aliens: *Why haven't they come and taken me again?*

Hooper laughs. He shakes his head. Takes a bite out of his burrito. Laughs again. Looks at me. Puts his long hand on my shoulder in a friendly way.

"I wasn't abducted," Hooper tells me.

"But you're in group," I say.

This is it. The moment where he's going to call me a fraud. Say what happened didn't happen. That it was just a dream. A made-up fantasy. A childish wish. I make a fist. I will punch him in the face if he says that. I will get into my car and leave him here to find his own way home.

"It seemed like the right place to go," he says, and then sprinkles some more cilantro onto his burrito.

"Why?" I ask.

"I thought you understood." He's looking at me like he's genuinely upset that I haven't gotten it.

"No," I say. "I don't."

"Mal, I am an extraterrestrial," he says.

"What?"

He points to the sky. "That star—you earthlings call it Epsilon Eridani. That's my star. All I want to do is get off this planet and go home. But although it hangs there in the sky, close enough for me to see with my naked eye, it's ten-point-five light-years away."

I don't say anything. I just burn up with that feeling where all the cells in my body are on fire. It comes back in a swoosh. I throw my burrito down on the table. My soda goes flying. My pants are wet. Hooper offers me a napkin. I refuse it.

I can't believe that Hooper is making a joke, because he doesn't seem to be the joking type. But there he is, sitting there across from me with a smile on his face. I want to punch him.

I get up and walk away.

On the way to the car, I punch a spiny succulent that's in my way.

It hurts, and that's the point.

When I reach the car, I collapse into my seat. I put the key in the ignition but I don't turn the car on. I sit there, my head reeling.

Part of me wants to drive away. Leave him here, like I would have if he'd made fun of me. But I would never actually leave him alone here. I would never abandon anyone. So I sit in the car, going over what he's just said. Even though I'm sitting down, my hands grip the steering wheel as though it's going to keep me from falling down. Because the ground is the sky, and the sky is the ground. That's how upside down I feel.

How will I drive home when the world has gone so topsy-turvy?

I laugh.

Then I laugh again.

"Mal, get a grip. Hooper is a crazy homeless man who thinks he's an alien," I say out loud to myself.

But I am thinking about his teeth. And about his long, weird hands. And about how he can speak Spanish. And his unnameable smell.

I am sure of one thing: If he is an alien, he's not one that I've already met.

"Eating makes me sleepy," Hooper says, sliding into the passenger seat next to me. He clicks his seat belt on and immediately falls asleep, leaving me with my mind racing.

I try to wake him up. I pinch him. I shake him. I tickle him. He just mumbles that this body makes him tired and forces him to sleep in order to digest.

Maybe it's for the best. Maybe *I* need *him* asleep so I can digest what he's said to me.

I turn the car on.

As I back up, with my arm over the passenger seat, I glance over at Hooper.

He looks peaceful. He looks kind. He looks good.

My father emitted that kind of goodness. But it wasn't the truth. Inside there was only darkness. If he had any good in him, he would have never done what he did to my mother and me. Or, at least, he would have cared about what he did.

Is Hooper a soul in a meat sack hiding a hideous dangerous alien being inside?

Is he in group looking for people to abduct?

Is he evil?

Worse.

Is he going to leave me, too?

He looks nothing like the aliens that I remember from what happened to me. I know humans that look more alien than Hooper.

38.

Even back in school, I can't stop thinking about what Hooper said to me about being an alien.

I can't put a finger on this feeling that I have.

Anger. Betrayal. Joy. Disbelief.

Hooper is or isn't an alien. He is or isn't a crazy homeless man.

Either can be true.

I punch my locker. Then I punch it again. The cuts on my knuckles open and start to bleed.

I see a couple of kids around me cringe. They scatter away from me, taking solace near the water fountain. They think I'm going to punch them next. They think that this is the day I'm going to go ballistic. They probably have their hands on their cell phones in their pockets, ready to whip them out and call 911.

But I'd hurt me before I'd hurt them.

I lean my head against the cool of the metal locker. The coolness seeps right down into my brain and I feel calm for a minute. Even though the bell is about to ring. Even though I am going to fail the history exam that I didn't study for. Even though my knuckles are bloody from punching the cactus last night after Hooper said what he said.

"Hey," Posey says. She's standing right next to me. Unafraid. She stands there with me the same way I see her mom stay with the feral animals. She is slow and careful with her voice and with her movements. The amount of time that it takes for her hand to move from her hip to her face to brush away a stray piece of hair is an eternity.

"We're fostering that dog," she tells me.

"What?" I croak.

"That dog you brought in. My mom brought her home."

"Oh," I say.

"My mom thinks she's going to make a great dog; she just needs to be acclimated to people."

I am glad for the dog.

39.

I am actually upset that I don't believe Hooper.

Which is a hard thing for me to process. I mean, how come I believe that I was abducted by aliens, but I don't believe that he could be one?

It seems like I should believe him. Otherwise, what is the truth?

I ride my bike over to the shelter. I have to ask Hooper about what he said.

About being an alien.

It's the first time that I've been to his room. It feels ridiculous to confront a man in a tiny studio with an orange bedspread, a cream-colored landline telephone, and brown curtains drawn closed to block out the bright California sun. I am talking about the universe and there is a mysterious stain on the carpet.

"What do you want to know?" he asks.

He looks much too calm to be an alien.

"Everything," I say.

"I do not know how to answer that question," Hooper says. "Can you be more specific?"

"Did your people abduct me?"

"My people don't bring people up, Mal. We only send people down."

"That's the answer of a person who is not really an alien," I say.

"Are you having trouble trusting me?" Hooper says.

He is sitting on his bed and I am sitting on the only chair in the room. His paisley-patterned secondhand-store button-down shirt clashes with everything, including how I think he should look if he weren't a liar.

"You look like a human and you don't abduct people," I say. Then I ask, "Do you know why the other aliens took me?"

"I don't know," Hooper said. "I don't know them."

I feel stunned. As though he should know. As though there's some kind of alien crossroads where they all get together and talk about the funny earthlings. Where they compare notes. Or do battle.

"Mal, let me tell you about my people," he says.

I am suspicious, but I am also all ears.

He goes on to say that his planet's technology is okay but not that great. They can go longer distances but not with large ships. They are interested in exploration and science.

I must look disappointed.

"The universe is very big," Hooper says.

He sweeps his hand to span the sky. I look up. And I swear that on his ceiling there are stars. Have I been stunned? Is he in my brain? I recognize the Big Dipper and Orion, distorted by the stucco.

"There are some stars," Hooper says. "And Earth is here."

He points to the wall next to the sink, where there are no stars. I notice on the bedside table there's a lamp, the kind you can get at Target that projects the night sky on your ceiling.

"We are standing on a tiny planet, orbiting a small, uninteresting sun, on an outer arm of the galaxy we live in," Hooper says.

He opens his silver bag and unfolds a star chart. The chart is alive with lights that blink and twinkle. There are things that rotate, and points that move slowly, almost imperceptibly, in the form of rocket ships.

He points to the stars on the ceiling and then to their corresponding spots on the star chart.

"Every star a sun. Many planets. Many are dead. Lifeless rocks with nothing, not even an amoeba. Some gaseous giants where no life, not even a creative or spirited life-form, could figure out how to survive there."

Next to some of the stars, there is a symbol. Along the bottom of the chart there is a string of them.

$$ \daleth \therefore \propto \text{,} \perp \bullet \neg \smallsmile \int $$

The symbols roll along blinking and changing, like a news ticker.

I run my finger along them. The symbols and the stars are slightly raised, like Braille.

I don't know if they are really moving. I don't know if I can trust my eyes. Or my fingers. Or my heart.

"All these stars, the ones with small symbols on them, life

is there. Some planets have a kind of life that is unfamiliar. We might not call it life. Bugs. Single-cell life-forms. Plant life. Even animals. I have stepped on some of those worlds. Observed. Never harmed."

Then he moves my attention to another symbol.

ζ

"All these symbols are the ones with life that thinks. The ones with civilizations. The planets that house a sort of life as we know it, planets with life-forms that speak and build and think and dream."

There are thousands of stars on the chart, but only twenty-seven stars with those symbols.

"One of those stars is the star that shines on the place where I live," I say.

"Sol," Hooper says, pointing to this one lonely star, far away from the others.

It's sitting there. Far-flung, away from anything else. Alone. Abandoned. In exile from all the other stars that have even simple life on the planets around them.

"That kind of life. That kind of heart. That kind of dreamer, it's rarer than anything." Hooper pushes the chart toward me. "You can keep that if you want."

It's too beautiful a thing to give to me. I would lose it in a pile of mess in my room. Or shove it in my locker at school with a tuna sandwich. Or leave it open to fade in the sun on the front seat of my car.

"This is the copy," Hooper says.

He hands me the star chart now, closing my fingers around it.

"No, I couldn't. I mean, what would I do with it?"

"I find it a pleasant thing to look at."

I fold up the map carefully and put it in my bag.

In my gut, I believe him.

40.

When she is a certain kind of drunk, my mother loses all of her words. But just because she has no way to express how she feels, it doesn't mean that she doesn't want to say something. She pulls a book off the shelf and she reads. Dramatically. Slurred. Tearfully. Hysterical. Sometimes it's poems.

> *I know that it is all*
> *a matter of hands.*
> *Out of the mournful sweetness of touching*
> *comes love*
> —ANNE SEXTON ("THE FURY OF ABANDONMENT")

Sometimes it's passages from books.

> *Gentle reader, may you never feel what I then felt! May your eyes never shed such stormy, scalding, heart-wrung tears as poured from mine. May you never appeal to Heaven in prayers so hopeless and so agonized as in that hour left my lips; for never may you, like*

me, dread to be the instrument of evil to what you wholly love.

—CHARLOTTE BRONTË (*JANE EYRE*)

Sometimes it's Shakespeare.

So many journeys may the sun and moon
Make us again count o'er ere love be done!
But, woe is me, you are so sick of late,
So far from cheer and from your former state,
That I distrust you. Yet, though I distrust,
Discomfort you, my lord, it nothing must.
For women fear too much, even as they love,
And women's fear and love holds quantity,
In neither aught, or in extremity.
Now, what my love is, proof hath made you know;
And as my love is sized, my fear is so:
Where love is great, the littlest doubts are fear;
Where little fears grow great, great love grows there.

—THE PLAYER QUEEN IN *HAMLET*

When I come home and find her reading aloud, I know that she's drunk. The kind of drunk that means there was an anniversary that I didn't know about. Or that she's gotten wind of some kind of news. Or perhaps she just had a bad day where everything, all the lies, all the broken promises, all the heartbreak, were too much for her to bear.

I should feel sorry for her. But when she's in the living room reading out loud and gesticulating and spitting out her words and chasing them down with the heavier stuff, like bourbon, I don't even say hello. Or ask her if she's eaten anything.

I go straight down the hallway, turn on my computer, put on my earphones, and kick some troll ass with Sameer and Mark online.

The whole time I'm thinking of the symbol on the map Hooper gave me.

How we think. How we build. How we live.

How this defines us.

How we are stars that can explode.

41.

I probably shouldn't have brought the star chart to school, and definitely shouldn't have opened it during free period, but I like to look at it every chance I get.

"What is that?" Posey is leaning way over. Her chair is tipping off its legs and I fear for her safety, so instead of covering up Hooper's papers, I open them up toward her.

Her eyes pop open. "Star charts!"

She scoots her chair closer to me.

I can smell her now. I always thought she would smell good up close, just from the way that she looks. She smells lemony. Her hair falls all over the place as she leans over the chart, oohing and ahhing.

I sneeze.

"These are beautiful," she says. "The real deal. Where on earth did you get these?"

I don't have to say anything, and she doesn't seem to mind that I don't. She keeps looking at the charts until the bell rings.

"Thanks for showing me those, Mal," she says. "I really like space."

"Me, too," I tell her.

I don't know. I'm blushing—not because of her, but because of how embarrassed I'd be if I told her I'd gotten the chart from an alien.

"I'm going to go one day for sure," she says. "It'll be cheap by the time we're adults."

"I've been," I say. "Nothing to write home about."

Posey looks at me and laughs. Not in a mean way. She thinks I'm being clever. Or maybe that I mean I've tripped on acid or something and imagined it, even though I don't do drugs and never would.

She touches my arm when she laughs. That makes me feel good. I touch her back. Lightly, on the arm.

She laughs again. I am embarrassed by the tenderness of the moment. So I get out of there as fast as I can. As I leave, I hear Suki and Natalie. They are asking all kinds of questions, and laughing, too. But not in the nice way. They laugh daggers.

They say things like, "Watch out, you'd better not get too close or else you'll be the first one he'll look for to kill when he shoots up the school."

Here's the thing that they don't know:

You never harm.

You just observe.

42.

Hooper and I are taking a hike up to the Mount Wilson Obser-
vatory. He has five bottles of water in his bag. He says that the
gravity of the planet makes him extremely thirsty all the time.
He says that water here tastes funny. He says that it smells weird,
too. I think the water is fine.

We get to the top of the hill and in front of us are picnic
tables. Behind them are some telescope arrays that are collecting
data from space. Hooper looks pleased.

"Wonderful," he says. "I love how you humans are always
watching and listening. Even though you don't actually watch or
listen in the right way."

I take a long sip of water. He always says things that almost
make sense, but if you think about them, make no sense at all.
Like he's a fake Yoda. But the more I hang out with Hooper and
the more I look at the map, the less I worry about whether he's
crazy or not and the more I believe him.

"Hooper, did it happen to me? Did they take me?"

"I don't know, Mal."

"But there are aliens. Out there."

"Yes. There are other life-forms in the universe. Some are intelligent. We are not alone. You are not alone."

"I feel alone," I say.

"There are over six billion people on this planet," he says.

That's not what I mean, but for all that Hooper does understand, there are some things he doesn't get. He wanders the universe, or so he says, alone, just him and the blackness of space, and the quiet of the suns, and the thoughts he has, as his companions.

But I need to know what happened to me.

"Look at me, Mal. I am your friend. I am not from this world. Therefore if you feel that you were taken, then I believe that it is very likely that you were."

"I need proof."

"You will never have proof. If your abductors are anything like my people, they want to be hidden. Secret."

"But I need to understand."

"You will likely never understand."

"Why?" I ask. Then, when Hooper doesn't answer, I ask him something else.

"Do you think we humans are so bad, that you're going to tell your people to enslave us or attack us or something?"

Hooper laughs.

"I'm not kidding," I tell him.

"Mal, I have shown you how Earth is very far removed from the center of this galaxy. It is a tiny planet far flung out away from anything. You are all likely to die out before your species learns how to even escape your own solar system. My people are not in the habit of exterminating or colonizing. We're explorers. We're scientists. We're interested in the beauty of life. There is not much beauty here, as advanced as you are. Your species is terrible. A terrible species. Selfish. Evil. Cruel."

"All of us?"

"No, not all of you. But there is so little hope here, I'm convinced every day that you will blow yourselves up."

"Why do you hate Earth so much?"

"*Hate* is a very strong word. I don't hate. I *dislike*."

"Okay, what is there to *dislike*?"

Although, when I think about it, I have a million things that I dislike.

"Do you really want to know?" he asks.

"Yes," I say.

"There are things in this universe that are evil. I'm surprised you don't know that. There is so much evil on this planet."

It is something I know, but it's the kind of thing I hoped wasn't obvious to aliens.

"Couldn't you preach peace or something? Couldn't you help us?"

If he could help us, then maybe he would help me.

"No."

"Why not?"

"Do you help ants?"

"What?"

"When you see an anthill, do you try to tell them what to do? Tell them where a better source of food is?"

"No," I say. "But we're not ants. Humans have a higher

consciousness. Humans have souls. Humans have opposable thumbs. Art. Literature. Infrastructure. Quiche."

"Burritos," Hooper says. "I am not saying that your people are barbarians. I'm only convinced that there is very little I can learn or do here that I want to learn or do."

"Detroit," I say.

"Pardon?" Hooper says.

"It's like Detroit. I went there once with my middle school. I used to be in chorus and we were competing there in the nationals. I walked around in Detroit. It was a perfectly fine city, but there was nothing about it that I liked or that made me want to know more about it. It didn't fit with me."

"That's exactly it," Hooper says. "I have been to more primitive planets and have had more of a connection. I've been to more sophisticated planets and have been dazzled by the heights of their civilizations. I think we can safely say that Earth is just not for me."

I think, *It's not for me, either.*

"I very much want to go home," Hooper says.

"Why don't you?"

"My ship was damaged upon entry," he says. "I may be here much longer than I ever intended to be."

"Isn't there anything you like about Earth?"

"You, Mal. I like you."

43.

Posey is waiting for me when I get out of the boys' room. I think it's kind of weird that she's waiting for me, but Posey is the type of person who doesn't really care if something seems weird. She does look like she's pretty excited and has to talk to me right away. I wonder if it's about the dog.

She shoves her phone in my face.

"What?" I say. I don't know what I'm looking at.

"Read," she says.

It's a news article about a civilian spacecraft that's going to blast off in a secret night launch from the desert in the next few days.

"So?" I say.

"I thought maybe we could go," Posey tells me.

"Why?"

"Because there's a spaceport right here in our own backyard, and I think it would be cool to go see something blast off into the sky."

I get a kind of vertigo feeling. I put my hand on the wall and lean on it, trying to look as cool as I can while also steadying myself.

Posey is standing there and looking at me. Other people are looking at Posey talking to me. Darwyn is fiddling with his bag near us.

I look back down at the screen.

For years, the desert in California has served as a spaceport for civilian attempts to reach the stars.

"My parents took me to see a rocket launch when I was younger," Darwyn pipes up. He's done what he does best—he's inserted himself into a conversation he wasn't having.

"I thought we could go," Posey says. "Anyway, we could go stargazing afterward. You know, make it a thing."

"I don't have any plans," Darwyn says. "I can bring food."

"Why don't you just go, then?" I ask Posey. I am not trying to be mean, but I have plans to go to my own space launch. And there will be no civilians involved. Except me, hopefully.

Posey cocks her head to the side as if to say, *Are you serious?*

"No one likes this kind of stuff but you, Mal," she says, spelling it out for me.

"I like a lot of stuff," Darwyn says. "I've been meaning to get into space stuff."

I realize that I always hear Darwyn saying that. He's always doing exactly what everyone else is doing. But he's never doing his own thing.

I give Posey back her phone.

"I'm pretty busy," I say.

Then I walk away.

44.

Hooper comes to me after I leave an Alateen meeting. He's standing at the bottom of the stairs at the community center. He's touching my bicycle and then pulling on his hair. He's agitated.

"Mal," he says. "I got a message. There is a mining ship near this solar system. They are willing to come get me."

That feeling. That feeling bursts inside of me. Hooper is going to go and I'll be alone again. It's like the sun setting. Like being condemned to eternal darkness.

"I want to go home," he says.

"That's great," I say. "So I guess this is good-bye."

"Will you help me go meet them?"

"Why do you want to leave here so badly?" I ask. "Why don't you just stay?"

"I'm all alone," he says.

And for all the alone he likes being, I realize that he's lonely. I know all about lonely and it's terrible.

When there has been a disaster, people seek out aid workers. Hooper might be alone, but for him it's a galactic-size crisis. And I'm his only hope.

"Okay. I'll help you."

45.

When they come, I'll ask him to take me with him.

46.

I've been looking at the map to nowhere that Hooper gave me, the map to the middle of the Mojave Desert. I am poring over it. Trying to see what possible place Hooper could imagine that the ship is telling him to head toward.

Everywhere in the Mojave seems like a road to nowhere.

But then I see something. It's not that far from the place that Posey talked about. The road he wants to be dropped off on is near the road that leads to the Mojave Air and Space Port.

I'm worried now that Hooper could just be crazy.

The only way to find out is to talk to him in person. Not in group.

Which is why I am hunched over the last working pay phone at school because Mom forgot to pay the cell phone bill again. I press the numbers on the keypad. I just hope he's in his room at the shelter to pick up and not out wandering around.

"Hello?"

"Hooper?"

"Mal."

"Yeah. We gotta talk."

"Not now. I'll call back in ten minutes."

I give him the number and he hangs up. Since he got word from the mining ship, Hooper has been acting strange. He's been sweating a lot. His temper has suddenly gotten short. And he's digging holes all the time.

The bell rings and classes let out. I figure I'll wait ten minutes and then I'll call him back. I go over to the nearest picnic table.

Kids come pouring out of class. They look like water. Or molecules. Or excited atoms.

"Hey." Posey is suddenly at full stop, standing in front of me. Suki and Natalie keep walking, failing to notice that she's not with them anymore.

Darwyn has noticed. He's at the next picnic table. He's tying his shoe. Eavesdropping.

"I just wanted to tell you that I have a telescope," Posey says.

"What?"

"I've got a really good telescope."

"For what?"

"If you're going out to the desert to stargaze or try to see that unannounced launch."

The halls fill to maximum capacity and then it ebbs, the flow of bodies going down from a steady stream to a trickle. To nothing. Doors close. Stragglers rush. I am a rock.

The late bell rings.

"You're going to be late for class," I tell her.

I think she's going to say something else to me, but all of a sudden the pay phone rings. I jump up to get it.

"Hello? Hooper?"

"Mal. Did you get the coordinates?" he asks.

"Yes. There's nothing there." *Except a civilian spaceport.* But I don't tell him that.

"That's the point," he says. "They are coming tomorrow night. I don't have much time. Can you get away from your educational obligations tomorrow?"

"Tomorrow? Sure. What time?"

"Eight thirty in the morning."

"I thought you said it was at night."

"I have some things to get on the way."

Which I think means he wants to dig some more holes. He's got a sack of rocks in his room. They don't look special. They look like regular rocks.

"Got it. Eight thirty. I've got to fill up the tank. Meet me at the gas station at La Cresta and Moore."

I hang up the phone and lean my head on the receiver.

There's only one thing left to do: pack my bags and figure out how to convince him that I want to go along.

47.

I'm extra nice with my mother that night. I don't know how long I'll be away. I don't know if I'll ever come back to Earth. Why would I want to? It's like Hooper says—humanity kind of sucks.

But I feel bad that she's going to be alone. I feel worried.

I make sure that the pantry is fully stocked with stuff, and the freezer, and the fridge. I know that she'll probably stop eating for a while when I go. So I got some nutritional booster drinks as well.

48.

I pull up to the gas station at seven because I want to make sure the car is in tip-top shape for our drive to the desert. First I fill up the tank. I check the oil and the transmission fluid and fill those. Then I fill up the tires with the perfect amount of air. I'm cleaning the windows when I hear another car pull up. I look up and I see Dr. Manitsky's veterinarian truck. She waves. I wave back.

I think she's just here to fill up her tank or something. I'm even thinking of asking her if she wants me to check her tires or clean her windows or something, when the side door opens and Posey comes out of the passenger side of the car, lugging a telescope. She's got a thermos in the other hand and a big backpack with a sleeping bag strapped to it. Dr. Manitsky waves again, and then pulls away, leaving me and Posey staring at each other.

"What are you doing here?" I ask.

"I heard your rendezvous time for the launch. I thought maybe you wouldn't mind."

I don't say anything.

"I brought my telescope, like I said I would."

The screen door of the house that's next to the garage slams. I look over and I see Darwyn jogging over to us.

"Did I miss it? I woke up late. Are we leaving now?" Then he looks from Posey to me. "Where is everyone else?"

"No one else thought rocket launches were cool enough," Posey says.

"And you guys aren't coming," I say.

I could stand here and argue with them all day. I could stand my ground. Actually draw a line in the sand.

But the morning is cut with the sound of whistling, a melancholy tune that we hear carried on the air. And then we see him, Hooper, like a mirage that's just appeared on the highway. He's walking with his long, skinny legs. He's got his silver backpack on. He's got a blue jumpsuit on. He's wearing a sun hat. The rising sun is behind him. So it looks like he's all aglow. He sees us all but he doesn't acknowledge us. He's staying in his own little world. Population One. Whistling his tune. Which he finishes as he steps up and joins our little circle.

"Is this everyone?" he asks.

Posey is the one who nods.

"I brought my telescope," she says, indicating the package under her arm.

Hooper gets right into the car, placing his backpack on the floor at his feet. He pulls out a fancy device and places it on the dashboard.

"I'll be the navigator," he says.

I put my hand up to stop Posey and Darwyn from heading into the car. I get into the driver's seat.

"Hooper," I say, "they don't know where we're going. They think we're going stargazing or something."

Hooper looks at me.

"It will be easier for you when I leave if you're not alone," he says. Then he rolls down the window and waves for Posey and Darwyn to come into the car. I reluctantly open the trunk for Posey to dump in her stuff, and then they get in the backseat.

As Hooper introduces himself to Posey and Darwyn—not mentioning the alien part, but saying he's a friend of mine— I curse under my breath and put the car into drive.

"Where am I going?" I ask.

Hooper turns on his little machine.

"North," he says. "Head north."

49.

I know what I have to do. I have to get Hooper alone, away from the others. And tell him about my plan.

I'll hitch a ride out of this place.

I'll get as far away as I possibly can.

I'm going to go see a new sun.

Step my foot on a new planet.

Make myself into a new kind of human being.

50.

Hooper is leading them in rounds that no one has ever heard of, so they are singing songs when it happens. First there is a sound, then the car goes a little wobbly and there's the sound of metal on asphalt.

"The tire's blown," Darwyn says.

"I know," I say.

"Better pull over," he says.

"I *know*."

I pull onto the shoulder. We get out of the car to survey the situation.

"Shredded," Darwyn says. "Unsalvageable. We'll need a new tire."

"Well, I have to change this one," I say.

He hovers there, like he wants to help, but this is a one-man job. I stare at Darwyn as I get the spare and the tire iron and the jack from the trunk, until he stops hovering and moves over to Hooper and Posey.

Posey is sitting on a rock. She's put on a huge pink hat. Darwyn has his hand on his hip. Hooper is sweeping the ground with his weird machine and is telling Posey and Darwyn the story of one time when there was a malfunction on a vehicle that he was driving. It sounds like he was driving in the Arctic or something. Not that he was in the dead of space.

The machine beeps, and he gets out his tiny garden shovel and starts to dig. Somehow, it seems like a perfectly normal thing to everyone. Like he's just looking for buried change.

I wipe the sweat from my forehead and get to work.

51.

"Look at this!" Hooper says.

Hooper keeps leaning over me, like his leaning is going to help me somehow, but instead, he's just kind of blocking the light, showing me a very tiny rock. I wave him away.

Darwyn and Posey are having a serious conversation. At first I tune them out, concentrating on the task at hand. But snippets of their conversation keep sliding in. So now I'm listening, even though I'm crouched on the other side of the car with the jack and I'm trying to get the bolts off the wheel. They're rusty.

"She was brain-dead when they found her," Darwyn says. "I was little. I slept through the whole thing. Imagine that? A car goes spinning around a bunch of times and I'm thinking that I'm just on a cloud or something."

Three bolts off. One more to go.

"I woke up when the sirens came. My mother just looked like she was asleep, so I don't remember being too worried. They put her on the gurney and took her away. She looked like a queen being carried away like that. Like a sleeping beauty. My dad came, and he was holding on to me and crying. I had never seen my dad cry before, so that was what scared me. The next day he came home, and sat me down, and told me that she wasn't coming back. That he had told them to unplug her and that she was dead."

Fourth bolt off. Wheel removed. I'm sweating. I might also have something in my eye. I look over at Darwyn, sitting on the side of the road with Posey. She's very attentive to him. Hooper is standing there, between us. Protective but also giving everyone space.

"So you never got to say good-bye?" Posey asks.

Darwyn makes a noise that sounds kind of like an elephant honking. It's not pretty, or sad, or mournful. It's just ugly. But it's full of feelings that I recognize. It's full of grief.

"They donated her organs. Someone's got her eyes, her liver, her kidney, her lungs, her heart."

"An act of beauty and kindness," Posey says.

"I hate when people at school call me the Lung," he says. "It hurts in a way that they can't possibly understand."

Posey starts to hold his hand. I'm a little jealous, but I brush that feeling away along with the sweat on my face. Hooper joins them.

I pull the wheel off. The force of doing it sways me off balance. I fall flat on my back with the wheel on my chest. I'm looking up at the sky. There's only one cloud. I'm winded, so I watch that cloud for a minute.

Darwyn continues. "I keep thinking that anyone walking around could have a part of her. And if I just found one person that had a piece of her in them, I could go right up to them, and I could say good-bye."

While I'm waiting to get my breath back, I'm thinking. I breathe in. I breathe out.

"You could do that," I say from my side of the car, the wheel resting on me. It's warm and heavy, like all the worries that I carry.

"What?" Darwyn says.

"I didn't even know you could hear us," Posey says.

"You could find someone, maybe a woman, about your mother's age, and just tell her that story. And then, you could look right at her heart, and you could say good-bye to her."

"Would that work?" Darwyn asks.

"Sure," I say. "Why not?"

"It won't be her heart," Darwyn says.

"It could be," I say.

"If they are a good human, they'll understand," Hooper says. "They'll take your love in. That's what I've come to understand about your species."

Darwyn doesn't say anything. He just gets up and dusts the dirt off his backside and takes the wheel off my chest. Then he finishes changing the tire like an expert.

"We need to get a real tire," he says, putting the tools back into the trunk. "This dummy wheel won't do for the rest of the driving. Good thing you have me along. I'll be able to put it on myself. It'll cost us less."

Posey gets up, and as she does, she catches my eye.

"You're nice," she mouths.

And what's funny is that I feel nicer. Even though I realize that I always feel this way.

52.

When we pull into Mel's Garage it looks deserted. But after pressing on the horn for a second, a mechanic comes around the side of the building.

"Can I help you?" the woman in coveralls asks.

"We need a tire," Darwyn says, taking things under control. He tells the woman the kind of tire that we need.

"I think I've got one of those," she says.

I notice that her name tag says MEL. She's about fifty. She's got blond and brown hair, like a rockabilly chick. When she turns to walk away from us, she swings. For an older lady, she's kind of sexy.

She disappears into the garage and then comes out rolling a tire. She rolls it right up to us. Darwyn inspects it and then says it looks all right. Then he gets to work jacking up the car.

Hooper pays for the tire with cash.

Once the tire is changed, I watch as Darwyn puts the jack carefully back into the trunk. He wipes his sweaty forehead and looks back over at Mel, who is sitting at a plastic picnic table, drinking an orange soda and talking on a cell phone. The orange is so bright against the color of the desert.

"Ready to go?" I ask.

"Yep," Posey says, opening the door.

We all get in, except Darwyn, who's staring at Mel.

"Darwyn?" I say. "Come on, let's move."

"Hang on a second," he says. He takes off his glasses and cleans them with the hem of his shirt. Then he squats down and looks in the side-view mirror and kind of cleans his face and runs his hand over his hair to smooth it a bit. Then he heads across the asphalt lot, over to Mel.

Mel looks up at him, kind of startled. We watch as he says something to her and she motions for him to hang on a second and then hangs up her phone. They start to talk. Darwyn is standing there and Mel is looking up at him, and just by the look on her face, and the way it changes, we can all tell what he's doing.

"Is he telling her?" Posey asks. "Oh my goodness. He's telling her."

Darwyn sits down. He puts his head in his hands. Then he puts his head on the picnic table. I can see his big chest heaving up and down. Mel has leaned over and she's rubbing his back.

From way over here, it's heartbreaking.

"I'm going to check in on him," Posey says. She scoots out of the car and heads over to Darwyn and Mel. When Posey reaches him, she puts her hand on his back, and he hugs her waist. And I watch as she leans over and whispers something to him. Then he gets up and heads with her to the bathroom.

This could take a while.

"Hooper, wanna take a walk?" I ask.

This is my chance to talk with Hooper.

To ask him to take me away from here.

53.

This is probably going to be my only chance to make my case.

While Posey helps Darwyn wash the crying off his face in the garage bathroom, I am finally alone with Hooper. We walk over to the edge of the concrete and step into the desert. We have our backs to the sun. We've been going north and west. But as we stand side by side, we're looking back to where we came from. Back toward the east.

"Do you know, Mal, that I didn't get to see very much of this planet?" he says. "I had so many plans."

"Well, you could come back," I say, even though I don't want him to come back, because I don't want to come back.

"I don't think so," he says. "Here is very far."

He turns around and looks up at the sun, gauging the time that's passing.

"Hooper," I say, and I wonder if that's even his real name.

I wish I knew the protocols of his planet. I'm irrationally worried that I should be using his real name when asking something so huge. Then again, maybe his real name is unpronounceable and that's why he uses Hooper. I want him to know how sincere I'm being. Then I'm excited that if he agrees to take me with him, I might get to know his real name. Learn his language. Know his ways.

"I want to come with you," I tell him.

He doesn't say anything. Instead, he kicks at the ground and starts digging at the dirt with his foot.

"Take me with you," I say, in case he didn't hear me.

But I know he did, because he stops playing with the ground and looks everywhere else but at me. I hear my heartbeat in my ears. I hear the wind. I hear a truck. I don't hear the answer that I'm waiting for. The answer that's going to set me free.

"Are you really in that much pain?" Hooper finally asks.

I want to tell him that I am standing here in the middle of the desert. It's hotter than the hell I feel I'm living in. And that I am willing to do anything to get light-years away from here. Even believe a man when he tells me he's from the stars.

Yes. I am in pain.

But saying a word like *yes* out loud, very casually, doesn't state my case strongly enough.

So I find myself standing on the edge of an emotional cliff where I know I'm about to be disappointed. *Again.*

I'm about to be left behind. Again.

I know about pain. And I don't think I can bear it.

I clench my hands into fists and I scream. I scream louder than the cars on the freeway. I scream louder than the shrill of the desert birds. I scream louder than every piece of air in my lungs.

"I can't take you with me," Hooper says.

"Please," I say. "Please take me with you."

I am down on my knees in the dirt and I am hugging Hooper's legs. I'm not even sure if he can understand my begging because I am sobbing great gulpy gasps. I need him to take me with him. I need him to be who he says he is. I am afraid that he's not. That makes me feel worst of all.

"Are you certain you are prepared to be alone for an eternity?"

I nod and sob, hoping it sounds like a yes.

"No one will come to get you where we are going. Every being will be different from you. You will be an orphan. All alone."

"I don't care." I manage to make the sentence sound coherent.

Hooper looks at me. He looks like he's going to say yes.

"I have spent months here on this earth, in despair. All alone. I have been around people who I do not understand and who do not understand me," he says.

"But that's how I feel right now," I say. I get up and I face him like a man. Like a human man.

"Mal, I cannot condemn you to the silence of the universe," he says.

"I've been taken before," I say. "I'm not scared. It won't be any different."

"Mal, it *will* be different," he says.

"It won't be."

"No one knows for sure that you were taken."

"*I'm* sure," I say. But really, I'm not sure of anything.

He doesn't go on. Maybe it's because he's taking the first rule of group seriously: Always support a fellow contactee's claim. It is their experience. And although it may be different from yours, it is their truth.

Or maybe he's being quiet because he's only a guy with a few screws loose. A guy who wanted a free trip to the desert. A guy just like anyone else.

"You cannot know what you are asking," he says.

I've come this far and I'm not going to give up.

"I do know what I'm asking," I tell him. "I do."

"You cannot. But as a traveler, I do. And because you are my friend—my only human friend—I must spare you from the harm that you are asking me to bring you."

"So your answer is no," I say.

"My answer is no," he says.

54.

I'm mad at Hooper when I get back to the car.

"What's wrong?" Posey asks. She's asking for real. Because there is something wrong. Hooper won't take me with him into outer space.

"Nothing's wrong," I say.

"Something is wrong," Posey says. "I'm your friend. You can tell me."

I look at her standing there. Her big, floppy pink hat. Her bright smile. Her great tits. And I struggle with the unfairness of the hand that I was dealt.

"The thing is, there's nothing wrong with you. You're perfect. You have a perfect life. Perfect friends. Perfect tits. You fit in perfectly."

Posey looks at me like I've said something dumb for the first time that she's known me.

I go on. "It is frustrating to talk to people who just don't get it. Who have it so easy. Who glide through life."

"I'm not perfect," she says. "I don't fit in."

"You do. Everything about you is perfect and I hate you."

I don't know where this is coming from. Or I do—it's coming from the fact that I'm stuck here. I shouldn't be directing it at her. I shouldn't be mad just because she fits in and I don't. I know this. The only way to stop myself is to get away from the car. So I pick a direction and I walk. But Posey runs and shoves me. She runs in front of me.

"Guys," Darwyn says. He sounds nervous. Posey shoves me again.

"Quit it," I say.

Her lower lip is trembling and her fingers are fiddling with the buttons on her sweater. She is contemplating something. Thinking really hard.

"I am not perfect. I don't have a perfect life. I don't have perfect tits," she says.

And then, her fingers fly as she unbuttons and pulls off her sweater, takes off her shirt.

She hesitates at her bra.

But we can already see that something is wrong.

"Stop," Darwyn says. "Don't."

She slides off her bra and it falls to the ground.

"I don't even have a nipple," she says.

Her head hangs down as she looks at her breasts.

I can see where she's imperfect. It is a burn, still holding on to the shape of a stretched-out triangle, and it ruins her perfectly unblemished skin. The scar is pink and mottled and angry and it ruins the line of her body.

Josh never touched those breasts like he said. I know that

for a fact. From the way she is standing there, trying to show us and trying to cover herself up. Probably no one has seen her burn.

"What happened?" Hooper asks. He asks in that gentle sing-song way he has about him. The one that gets right into the parts of you that are warm.

"I was little. I don't remember. I was three. My mom says I was running. I was naked. I ran into the ironing board. The whole thing fell on me, and my mom said that I sizzled. I cooked, like I was a pressed sandwich. She pulled it off me and she said that most of my skin came off, too. She said it was the most disgusting thing she'd ever seen."

Posey's crying. She's stopped walking. We all have. She's crying. I think Darwyn's crying, too. I look at the ground and feel like an asshole.

Darwyn and Hooper go to her side and help her back into her shirt.

I try to think of something to say. But I'm not good with words when I want to be.

"I'm not perfect," she says. She says it to everyone, but I know that she's saying it to me. And I really hear it. And I am sorry.

But I can't say it.

Even though she understands the way I am.

No one has ever said *I'm sorry* to me. So maybe I don't know how to say it, even if I feel it. Instead, I look up at her and try to tell her with my eyes. I hope she understands how much I mean it.

I am owed so many apologies that I don't know how to give one myself.

"Come on," I say after a bit. "You should ride up front with me."

We go to the car. We roll down the windows to let out the desert heat.

Posey holds the map on her lap; the pages settle and fall between her knees. I have my hand on the stick and shift it into gear as we roll faster down the highway. I steal three glances at her and then put my hand on the seat next to her hand.

I am too scared to take it.

But I am lucky that she is brave. She closes her fingers around mine in a friendly way.

Apology accepted.

55.

I see the sign. VICTORVILLE, 5 MILES.

Victorville. The town where my dad ended up.

"Let's pull over here and get something to eat. You must all be hungry," I say. "I know I am."

I pull the car into the parking lot of Al's Diner. We're the only customers in there, except for some guy sitting on a stool at the counter eating a grilled cheese sandwich. The sign says to seat ourselves, so we grab some menus and slide into a booth. I take the window. I want to see the town. See what it looks like. Try to understand what was so much better about here than there.

All I see is brown and dirt and squatting trees. Nothing too special. I press my fists into my eyes until I see blue. I don't open them again until the waitress puts the water glasses down in front of us.

I look at the menu.

I know I'm hungry, but I've lost my appetite. What if I see him here? What if he comes in on a break from whatever he is doing? What if he saunters over, just thinking that we're new in town. Passing through. Tourists. And he wants to make small talk, or something, just to be polite. To make pleasant conversation. I've seen him do that before. Always making the checkout girl laugh. Always looking like he was such a good guy. He just couldn't do that with the people who loved him best. With us, he was cold and guarded. But as soon as anyone else was around, he'd light up the room.

I think of something worse, too. It's such a bad thought that it makes me sick in the pit of my stomach. What if he does all that and comes in here and chitchats and doesn't even know that it's me?

Everyone else orders. And then it's my turn, and I'm trying to act like I have it all together. Even though I don't. Even though I think I might throw up. Even though I'm sitting here with two strangers who are laughing because they are excited to be on a road trip, even though they don't know where we're going or what we're doing, and an alien who's asking the waitress strange questions, making him look like he's crazy.

"How many pounds of beef do you have here?"

"Do you prefer sunny days or gray days?"

"How many pieces of that pie do you think you could eat?"

"Do your children understand your speech impediment?"

The waitress just answers as best she can. Like she's dealt with crazy people before and she's been there, done that, and it doesn't bother her one bit.

I order a veggie burger.

"Do you know a man named Harland Leighter?" I ask when she comes back with the food.

That kind of throws her and she curses under her breath.

"Harland?" she says. "You know him?"

I don't say yes or no. I just twist the water glass around.

"Figures," she says. "You must be here to see the play."

"What play?" I ask.

"Oh, he's the director of our community theater," the waitress says. "They've got a rehearsal of *Our Town* going on right now. You just missed him."

"I'll have a Coke," I say.

I know where he is.

She walks away shaking her head. And I know, for sure, that whatever it is that he does, he's done it to her.

"Who's Harland?" Posey asks.

I eat.

"Is that your dad?" Posey presses.

I don't talk.

Posey takes her hand and slides it over to mine and touches it lightly.

"Does he live here?" she asks.

I look up at her.

"How long has it been since you've seen him?" she asks.

There is something terrible about eating a veggie burger and having a private moment with yourself where you are trying to figure out what you are going to do. Like you're standing at the edge of a cliff and there's water underneath and a posse chasing you and you have to figure out if you can jump and live or stay and fight. Either way, whatever you do is going to hurt. It's bad enough to be dealing with that, but it's worse when you have three people staring at you, trying to figure out what's going on in your brain.

"Your father," Hooper says. I never told him about my father. It wasn't the kind of story I thought put humans in a good light.

"I don't want to talk about it," I say. I'm not even sure if it's true or not.

Posey and Darwyn try to hold up the conversation for the rest of the meal, and Hooper starts asking them strange questions, too. I'm not a part of it. I'm somewhere else, and they let me stay there. Eventually, I head to the bathroom to breathe for a second. When I get back, we pay the bill and get out of there.

"Shall we walk?" Hooper says. "Perhaps stretch our legs for a bit?"

I look up and down the street. I don't want to be here in his town and not confront him. I want to ask him the questions that I've had for years.

"What did you do to us?"

"Why would you abandon us?"

"Where is your heart?"

Or maybe just punch him.

"Do you want us to come with you?" Darwyn asks.

"Excuse me?"

I say it rudely. So rude that Darwyn starts to stammer.

"I just thought, maybe you might need someone to back you up. Or something."

"Why would I need that?"

"I filled them in while you were in the bathroom," Posey says. She says it slowly and carefully so that I understand it was not a betrayal but just a filling everyone in so that they can all help.

I can only imagine what she said. *Oh, Mal's crazy parents. The drunk and the sociopath. Imagine what he's going to turn out like.*

Except it's Posey, so she wouldn't say it like that.

"I don't want anyone else there," I say.

I don't want anyone to see that I might chicken out.

We agree to meet back at the diner in thirty minutes.

Hooper grabs my arm before I head out in my direction.

"Mal," he says.

And then he looks at me like he wants to warn me, or impart some kind of wisdom. Like maybe he's going to use some kind of Jedi mind trick to keep me from doing something crazy.

But then he doesn't. He just lets go of my arm and walks away from me. Whistling.

He does that because he trusts me.

56.

There's an American flag whipping around in the wind on its pole in front of the town hall. It looks faded because the desert sun is so strong. I see a rattler slither by in front of the sign in the glass that says VICTORVILLE COMMUNITY PLAYERS PRESENT *OUR TOWN*. A truck is pulled up, loading in some gear. I see a man whose stance I recognize.

My dad.

I wonder what I'm going to do.

Am I going to confront him?

Am I going to punch him?

My heart is beating wildly. It's totally out of my chest. It's flopped onto the ground and it's beating its way all over to the guy. He sees me and waves me over. I follow my heart and head over to him. When I get there, my heart jumps back into my chest.

He looks at me. He looks *like* me.

"Lend us a hand? We need to bring this table in."

I take a corner of an old antique table with my dad and two other guys. We bring it into the hall. Decide where it should go and then head back outside into the blast of desert heat.

Everything looks a little bit wobbly, the way that things do when it's hot.

My dad wipes his brow.

"Thanks," he says, extending his hand to shake mine. I ignore it. He seems a bit put off. I see some anger flicker across his face. His face is different. More lines. More gray in his hair. More worry. Or maybe it's that he looks like he's wearing a mask. Or like he's a shell of a person. Not really real.

And is he smaller? He looks smaller.

I still don't say anything.

This is the moment. I think.

"I could pay you forty dollars if you stay and help unload the truck. We really need the help," he says. "I've got to go pick up my daughter from day care. My wife thinks it's my job."

I want to tell him that it *is* his job. To care for a child. To show up.

"I gotta go," I say. "I gotta move on."

"Fair enough," he says.

So I do it.

I turn around.

I walk away.

I'm wrecked, but I'm also one million times lighter.

It's better to be the one who's leaving.

57.

When I rejoin them at the car, they don't say anything. They keep talking among themselves. I sit there, leaning against the car. Letting the waves of feelings roll off me.

I am fluctuating between feeling like I want to throw up and being happy about walking away. Maybe the unknown-ness, of letting it all go, is exactly like shooting off in a rocket headed for the stars. Maybe my heart is already in orbit.

So much of this isn't going the way I expected.

Hooper seems to really like Darwyn and Posey. They're all getting to know one another in an easy way. Hooper tells them both how I got him a place to live. Posey tells Hooper how much her mother respects my care for abandoned animals. Darwyn says how I always have a nice word for him at school. I know that they're talking about me, but it doesn't feel as though I'm the person that they're talking about.

"Actions," Hooper says. "Actions are the true words of humans. Words can be said or written and they can seem so beautiful. Seem so true. But I have noticed that a human speaks much louder with his or her actions and not with their words at all."

"What is it like where you're from, Hooper?" Posey asks.

She asks it like she thinks he's from another country. Like he'll say Albania. Or Zimbabwe.

Darwyn stares at Hooper while Hooper thinks about his answer.

"Where I am from, words match actions. All of the environment works together. We think of the long goals and not the short ones. We never lie. But sometimes that can cause great pain. But where I am from, the truth is much better served. Consequences are weighed very carefully."

"How so?"

"You have a game here. I have played it at the shelter. Chess."

"I love chess," Darwyn says. "I'm very bad at it."

"In chess, you have to consider a few moves ahead. What the action and the reaction will be. You observe before you act. Here it seems as though you act before you observe."

58.

Everything is taking longer than we think. Darwyn wants snacks. Hooper is interested in a mound of dirt. Posey needs to use the restroom. It's late afternoon and we're still in Victorville and the winter sun is setting and I couldn't be more glad to have the day leaving me behind.

The sky is orange and pink and purple. There are some incoming clouds that make every color reflect every other color. It looks like that migration map. I am filled with a longing for the sky and its promises. The swirl of color mirrors my confusion about what I want and where I am.

I wish a storm were coming.

59.

We see it before we hear it. It's right on the edge of town. The house is pulsating with color in the desert. Then the bass of the music hits us. It's a house party. People are lingering outside of the crap-looking prefab house. They hold red plastic cups. There are blue Christmas lights in the window. There's a keg stuck in the dust.

Cars are parking in the front yard. And I don't know why, maybe because I'm tired and I want to stop, but I pull over.

"What are you doing?" Hooper asks.

"I don't know," I say.

"It's a party," Darwyn says, stating the obvious.

"I don't want to miss the launch," Posey says.

I look at Hooper. Hooper shakes his head. Posey looks at me.

"We still have some time," I say. "We're not that far away."

We get out, and no one looks at us like we're weird or like we don't belong. No one here belongs. They are all hip and punk and crazy. The music is blasting from inside, and it's more than just an iPod mix. It's a live band.

Once inside the house, Hooper's face lights up, and for the first time since I've known him, I would say that he looks happy.

Here we are at a party where we don't know anyone. And we join the crowd standing in front of a band that consists of two keyboards, a saxophone, a stand-up bass, a drum kit, and a guitar.

A girl is singing into the microphone. She's wailing. She's got on heart-shaped sunglasses and a glittery miniskirt.

The bodies are moving all around us. Jerking this way and that. The bass player in a yellow shirt jumps so enthusiastically from side to side that it's a miracle he doesn't just throw himself right on the floor.

I feel the bass and drums right through my body. People are screaming. Pumping their fists in the air. Even I am. I look over at Posey and she's screaming, too. Laughing and singing. The tune is infectious. And I think I'd like to kiss her. And I think that Hooper might not be an alien. And it doesn't matter. It's not scary that he is or that he isn't. Because everyone here is an alien. Posey with her burnt boob. Me with my dark cloud. Darwyn with his sad brown eyes. That girl over there with the blue hair. Or that dude with his beltless pants showing his butt crack. Or that older woman with the tattoos on her face.

And all that matters is this moment and the sound that's in it.

60.

Before we reach the car, I stop. They deserve to know.

"I have to tell you guys something," I say.

"What?" Posey asks.

I look at Hooper. Maybe he's an alien, or maybe he's not. I don't need to out him as a faker. Just like he would never deny me what I think happened. But Darwyn and Posey, they deserve something closer to the truth.

Truth is truth is truth is truth.

"We're going to a space launch—it's just not the one you think we're going to."

"But we're on the road to the Mojave Space Port," Posey says.

"I don't understand," Darwyn says.

"I'm an extraterrestrial," Hooper says. "And I'm meeting a spaceship in the desert to hitch a ride home."

He points to the sky.

Posey swears under her breath.

"So there is no civilian space launch?" Darwyn asks. "I'm confused."

"No, there is one," Posey says. "I have the info here on my phone."

"We're just not going to that launch," I say.

"Is this some kind of joke?" Posey asks.

"No," Hooper says. "I don't joke. I am an alien."

"I don't know if I believe you," Darwyn says. "You look human. Statistics imply that alien life will be alien."

"That's fair," Hooper says. "But the rendezvous is very soon. Either it's true or I'm lying. But I have to be there."

"Did you know?" Posey asks me.

I nod.

"And you didn't tell us?" she says.

I shrug.

"What is wrong with you?" she says. "We need to talk."

She waves me and Darwyn over. Hooper starts to join us.

"Alone," Posey says.

Hooper hangs back and we three walk out of earshot.

"He wants to go home," I say.

"There's no such thing as aliens," Posey says.

"Yeah, statistically, it's not very encouraging," Darwyn chimes in. "It seems more and more likely that we are alone."

"I don't believe that's true," I say.

"You think Hooper is really an alien from outer space?" Posey asks.

"I don't know," I say. "But he might be."

"I might be a secret princess, and Darwyn might be the reincarnation of Einstein," Posey says.

Darwyn guffaws.

"I believe that aliens have visited us," I tell them.

"There's no proof of that," Darwyn says. "Rumors. Speculation. Conspiracy theories. But no proof."

This is the moment. I look up at the stars.

It's impossible to be out in the desert and not stare up at the stars. They dot the night. They twinkle. They hang like jewels. Every star a sun. Every single one.

"I was taken," I say. "Four years ago, I was taken."

It hangs there between us. My truth. Told not to a group that is predisposed to believe me. Not to a man who thinks he's an alien. But to two people.

"Oh, Mal," Posey says.

For a long time, no one says anything. Darwyn gets more and more uncomfortable the longer the silence goes on. He shifts on his feet.

"Okay, what if he is?" Posey asks.

"All we have to do is drop him off at these coordinates," I say.

"That's it," she says.

We all look over at Hooper. He gives us a little wave. We all wave back.

"You realize that he's probably just a crazy person?" Posey says.

"Aren't we all a little bit crazy?" I ask.

"I don't mind," Darwyn says. "We're already out here."

"What if he is an alien?" I ask. "And just because we think he's crazy, we blow his chance to go home."

"Mal, you need help," Posey says.

"It's important to me, Posey," I say. "I need to see this all the way through."

"Okay," Posey says.

We're going to drive into the middle of the desert, on a tiny dirt road, to bring Hooper to the end of the line.

61.

Hooper looks nervous as we walk toward him, so I smile to try to make him feel comfortable.

There isn't that much to say in the car. We're all lost in our thoughts. There's no moon. The desert is dark.

Hooper is the first one to speak as he begins to navigate us off the main highway and onto a small dirt road. The more turns we make, the more excited he gets, but as I glance in the mirror, I can see that Posey is becoming more worried.

Finally, we reach a sign that simply says ROAD ENDS.

"Here it is," Hooper says. "You can let me off here."

"Here?" I ask. "Are you sure?"

"There's nothing here," Posey says.

"Good place to land a spaceship," Darwyn says.

"The road is finished. We can drive no farther," Hooper says. He gets out of the car and we all follow him.

"Well, good-bye, then. And thank you," he says.

"We're going to take you," I say. "We're not going to leave you to wait alone."

"I must be alone, or they won't come," Hooper says.

"*Right*," Posey says. "Well, we'll leave you, then. Good-bye, Hooper. Nice meeting you. Have a good trip."

"Good-bye, Posey. Good-bye, Darwyn."

Darwyn looks kind of sad as he slides into the backseat of the car.

I'm standing with Hooper and I don't know how to say good-bye. It's not so easy for me as it is for them.

"Thank you," I say to Hooper. He doesn't ask for what. He knows that I needed him. To listen to me. To let me be weird.

"I'm sorry," Hooper says. "I hope you understand."

And then, without a big to-do, not even a hug, he turns and walks into the desert.

As he leaves, I see him for what he really is — a man with a kind heart who cannot bear this world, just like me. He's probably a little bit mentally disturbed — just like me.

I watch him walk until the darkness swallows him up.

62.

As we're driving away, putting distance between us and the end of the road, the darkness in front of us lights up.

A sign flashes by us—MOJAVE AIR AND SPACE PORT, NEXT EXIT.

Lifting out of the sky in front of us is a rocket, like an arrow heading straight into the sky. It's beautiful and the night lights up and the whole of the white ship is dotted with colors.

"Stop the car! Stop the car!" Posey says.

I pull over and we scramble out so we can all see it disappear into space.

"We can't leave Hooper there with no water," I say. "We have to go back."

We jump back in the car and I do a U-turn and step on the gas, listening to the GPS voice tell me how far I am from my destination.

"Hurry," Posey says.

"I'm going as fast as I can," I tell her.

"You have arrived," the GPS voice says.

I grab the flashlight I brought with me and run out of the car.

"Hooper! Hooper!"

We're all yelling.

"Hooper!"

"You guys stay by the car," I say. "I'll head in a bit."

"Be careful," Posey tells me. Her voice is genuinely worried.

I walk out into the desert, scanning the ground for tracks. I see something that looks like it was made by a human. I follow.

My flashlight flickers out. I bang it with the palm of my hand. It doesn't go back on. Dead.

It's black and I can't see the car anymore. It's so black that even with my eyes open it looks dark. There is no moon. The sky is now covered with clouds. I hear the wind.

I stop walking.

I close my eyes.

Something is happening to me.

I feel warmer than I've ever felt in my life. Warm like a bath. Or a blanket. I open my eyes. And I am looking at the planet Earth through a window. It is hanging there in the sky like a blue jewel. The landmasses look exactly like they do on a globe, only real. There are clouds forming over Africa. A clear day for most of North America. Antarctica is impossibly white.

A hand, if I can call it that, rests on my shoulder in a familiar way. And there is that weird animal smell.

Hooper.

I turn around.

The thing in front of me is translucent.

It cocks its head to the side.

I understand in my mind what it's trying to tell me. I can stay if I want. I can leave and go away from here. I can leave all my sadness behind.

My dad's words ring in my ear.

Are you ready for an adventure?

Yes, but.

Yes.

But.

Space, when you have more of it than you've ever dreamed of, is bigger than anything you can imagine.

But.

Yes.

I want to say yes.

I consider everything that I would leave behind. I can see it. It hangs there in front of me like a blue jewel.

It strikes me that a heart can be blue and still live. A heart can be blue and, with enough time, can warm again.

I am hit by the enormity of it all.

I *feel* it.

Back down there, in the desert, Darwyn and Posey are waiting by the car.

Back down there, in a town in California, a mother will be worried.

Back down there, in a country called America, a person is needed.

Up here, in space, this human decides to go back.

Back down there, to live on a planet called Earth.

Or, as I like to call it, *home*.